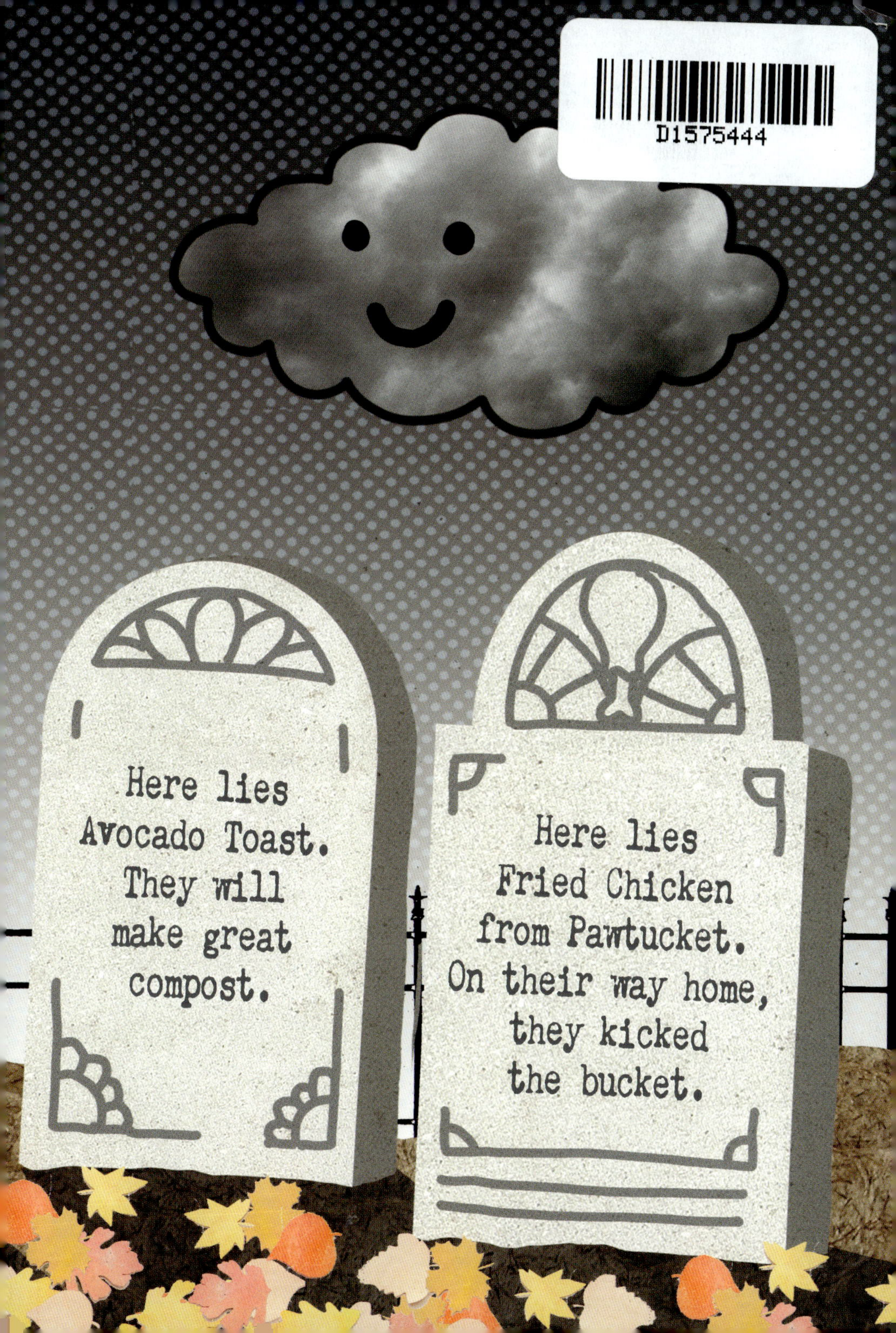
Here lies
Avocado Toast.
They will
make great
compost.
Here lies
Fried Chicken
from Pawtucket.
On their way home,
they kicked
the bucket.

You know you want to read ALL the Pizza and Taco books!

WHO'S THE BEST?

BEST PARTY EVER!

SUPER-AWESOME COMIC!

TOO COOL FOR SCHOOL

ROCK OUT!

DARE TO BE SCARED!

WRESTLING MANIA!
(COMING IN JANUARY 2024)

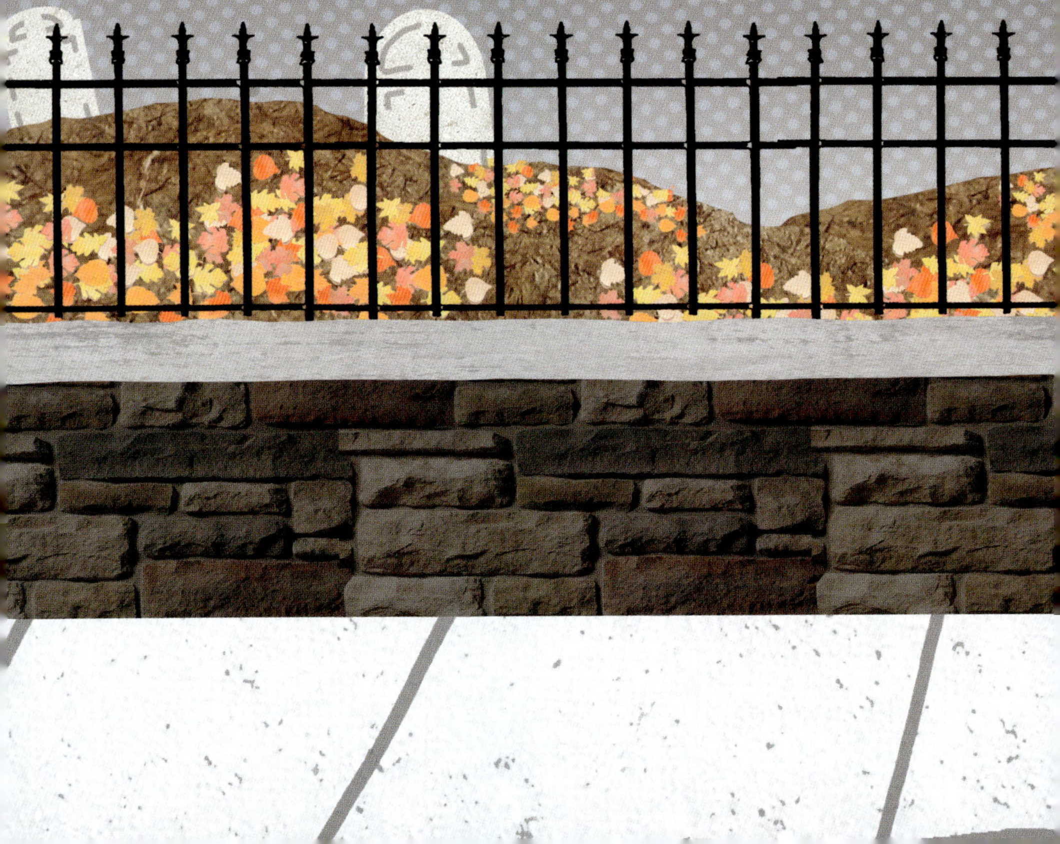

Pizza and Taco

DARE TO BE SCARED!

STEPHEN SHASKAN

A STEPPING STONE BOOK™

Random House 🏠 New York

This book is dedicated to Scott R.

Published in the United States by Random House Children's Books, a division of Penguin Random House LLC, New York.
Random House and the colophon are registered trademarks and RH Graphic with the book design is a trademark of Penguin Random House LLC.

Visit us on the Web! rhcbooks.com
Educators and librarians, for a variety of teaching tools, visit us at RHTeachersLibrarians.com

Library of Congress Cataloging-in-Publication Data is available upon request.
ISBN 978-0-593-48128-8 (trade) —
ISBN 978-0-593-48129-5 (lib. bdg.) —
ISBN 978-0-593-48130-1 (ebook)

MANUFACTURED IN CHINA
10 9 8 7 6 5 4 3 2 1
First Edition

Contents

Chapter 1
Get Scared

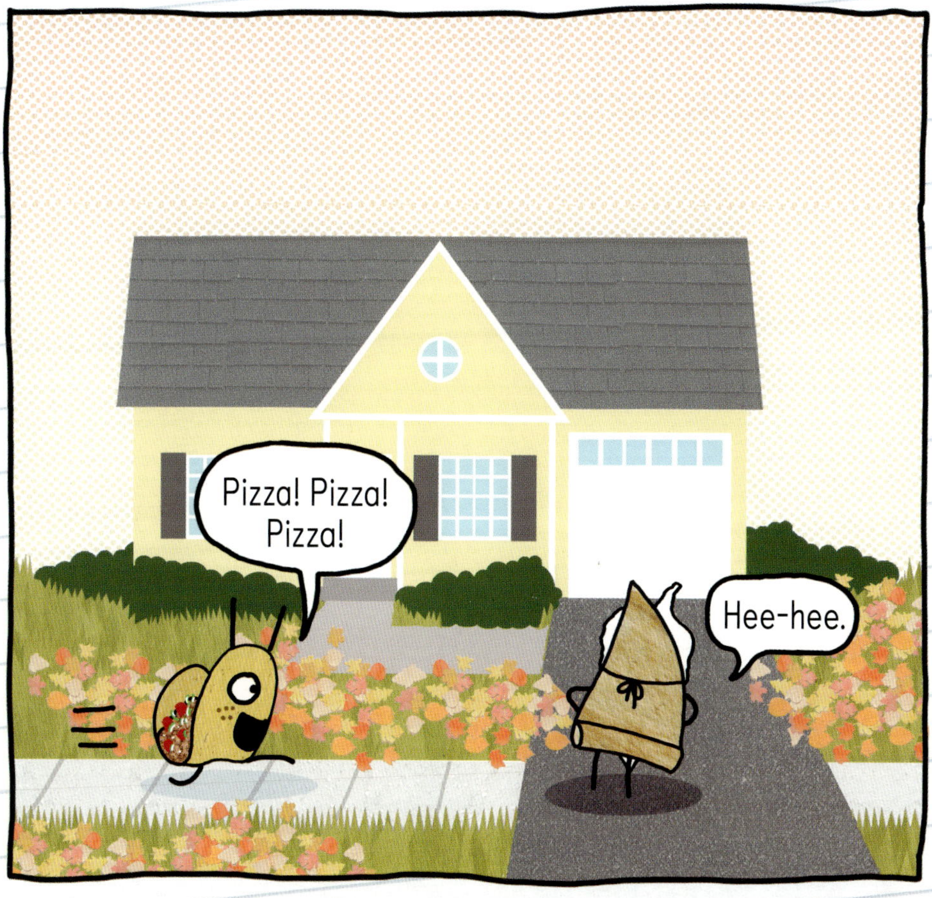
Pizza! Pizza! Pizza!
Hee-hee.

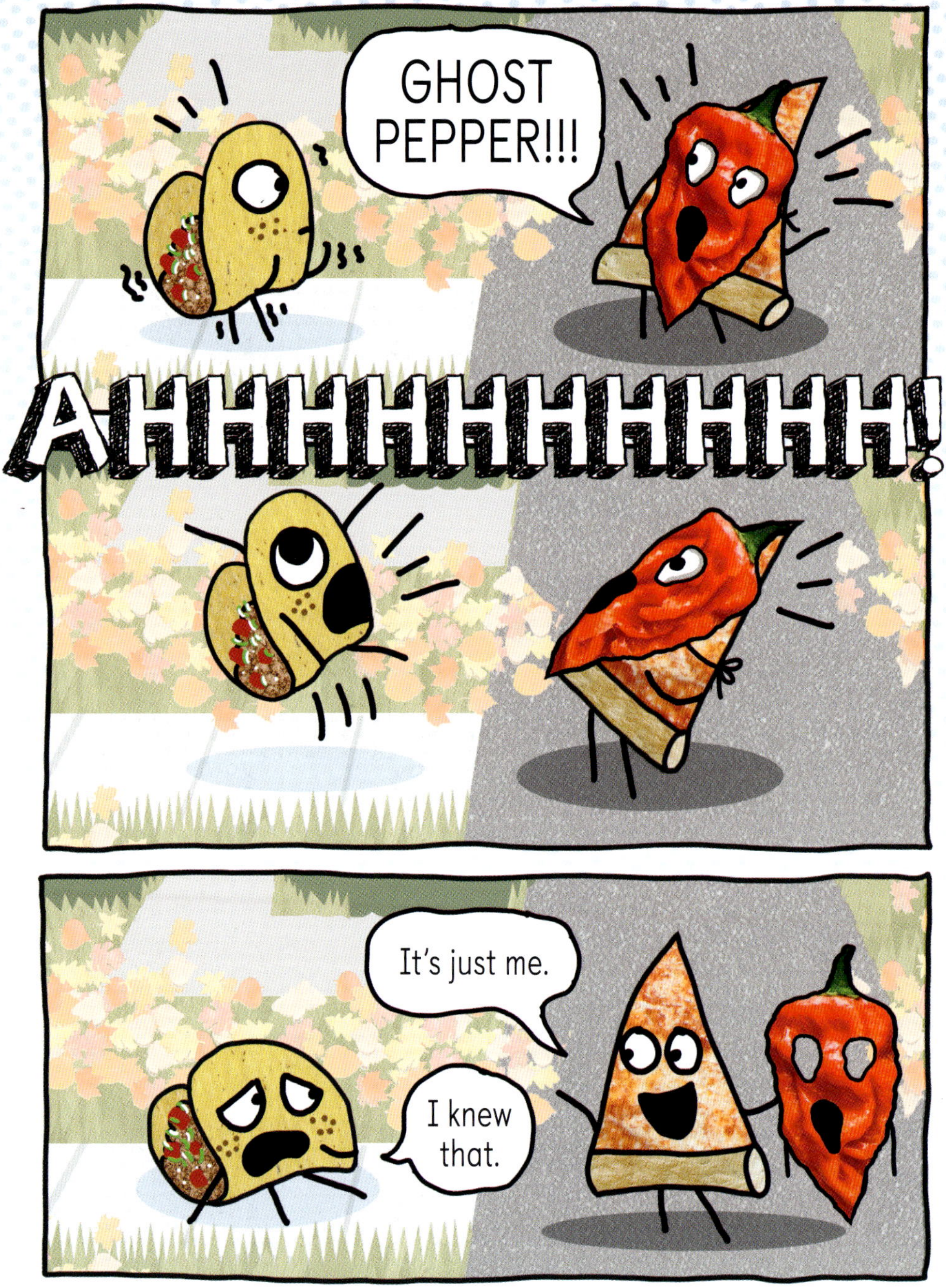
GHOST PEPPER!!!
AHHHHHHHHHHHH!
It's just me.
I knew that.

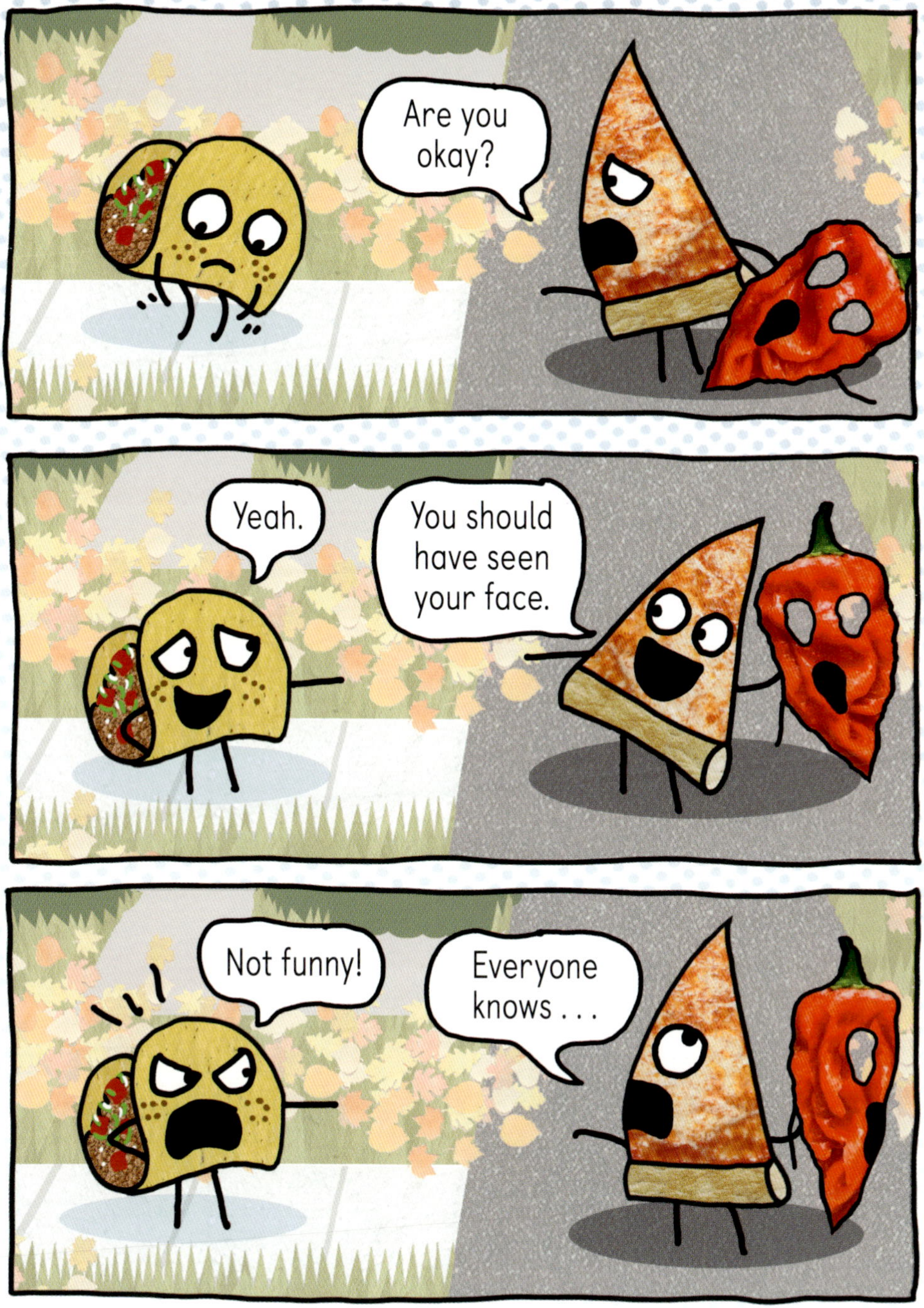
Are you okay?
Yeah.
You should have seen your face.
Not funny!
Everyone knows . . .

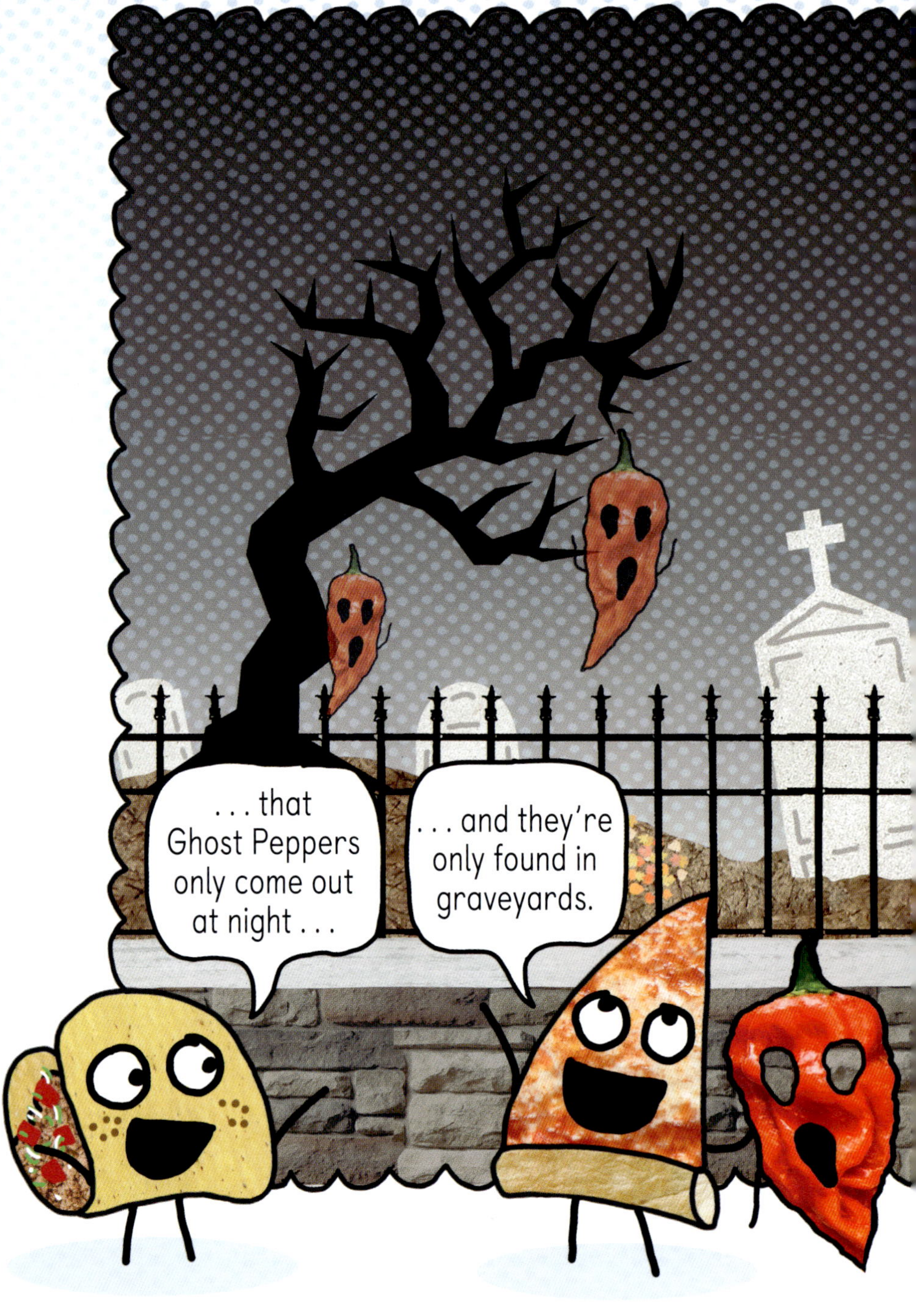
. . . that Ghost Peppers only come out at night . . .
. . . and they're only found in graveyards.

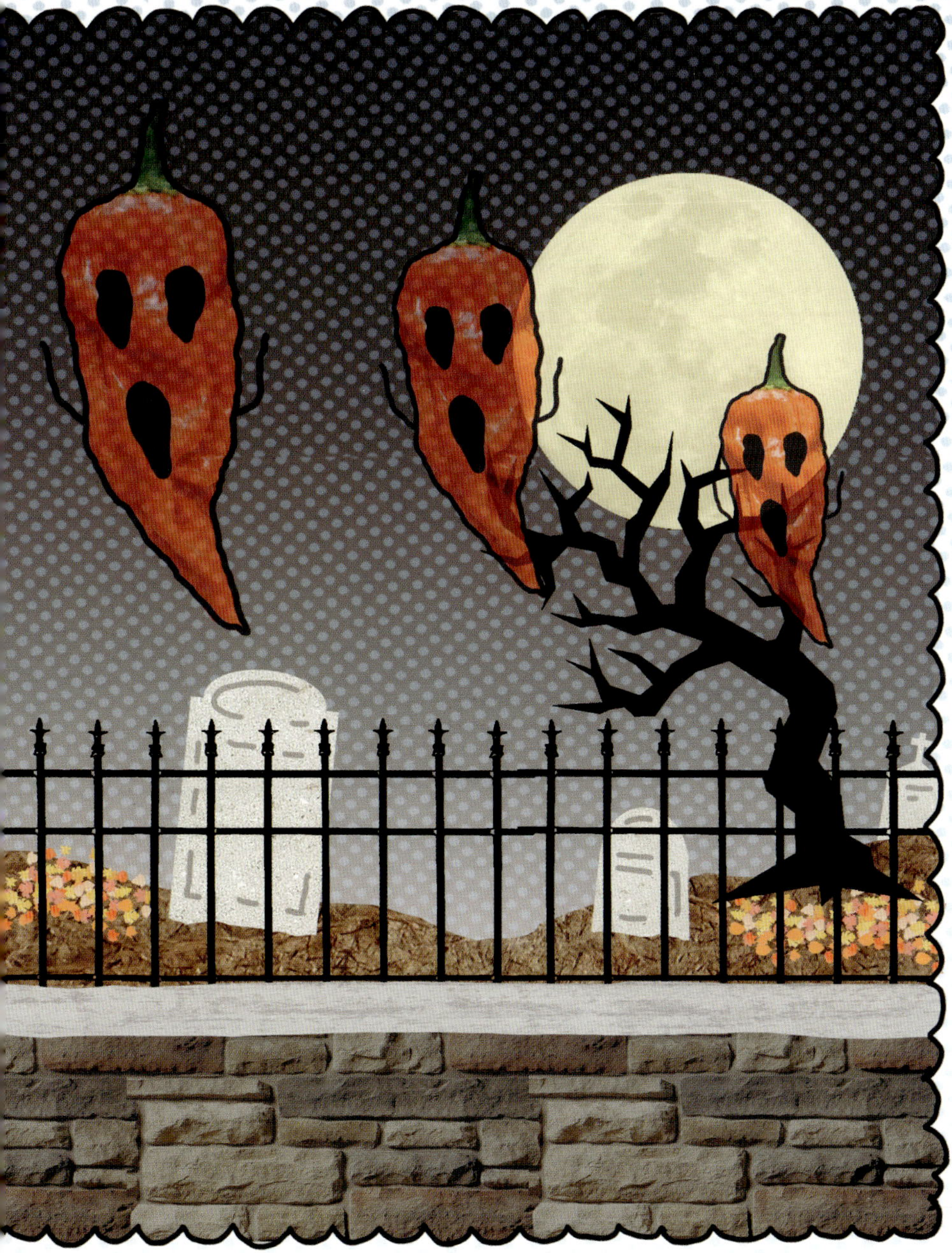

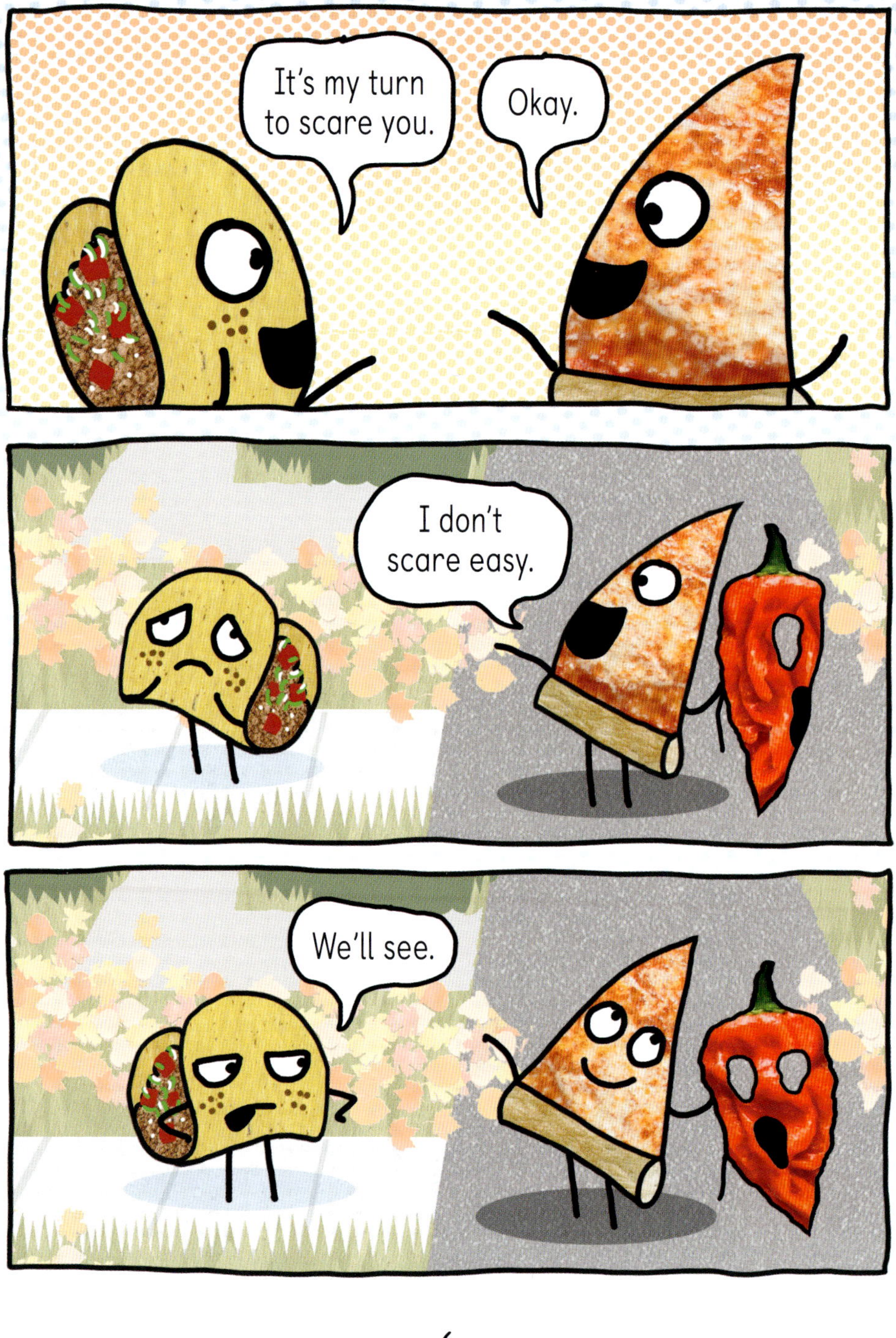
It's my turn to scare you.
Okay.
I don't scare easy.
We'll see.

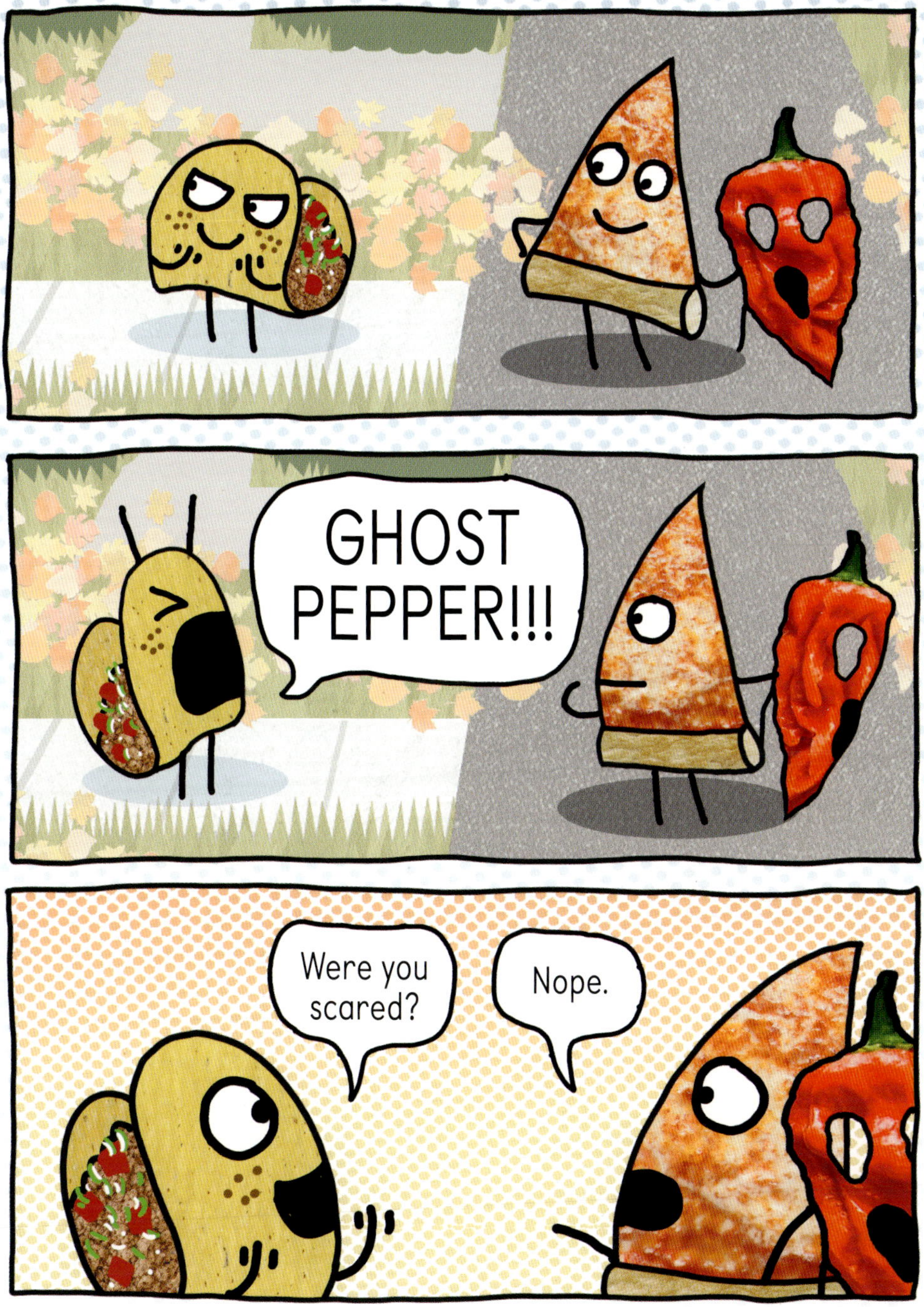
GHOST PEPPER!!!
Were you scared?
Nope.

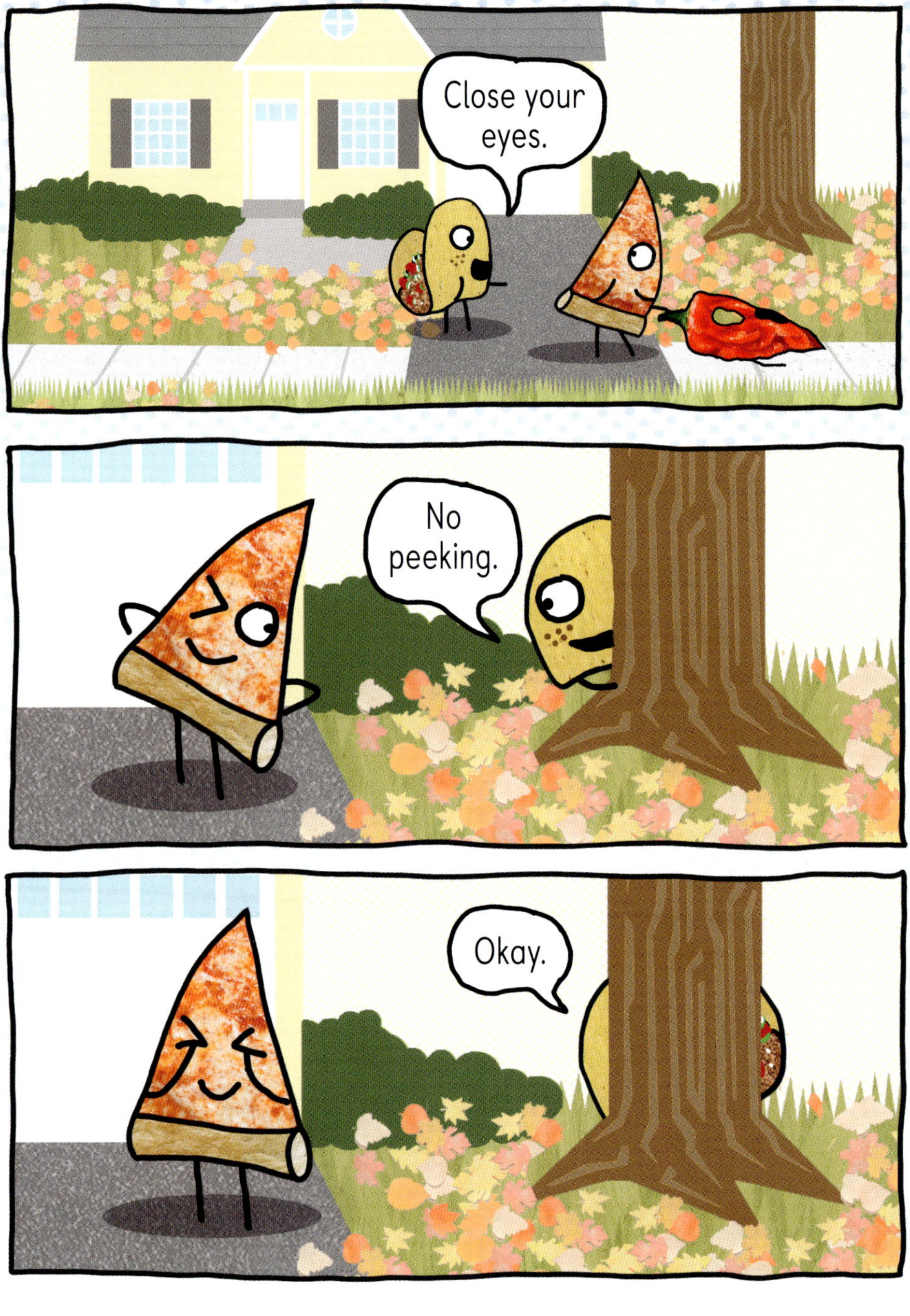
Close your eyes.
No peeking.
Okay.

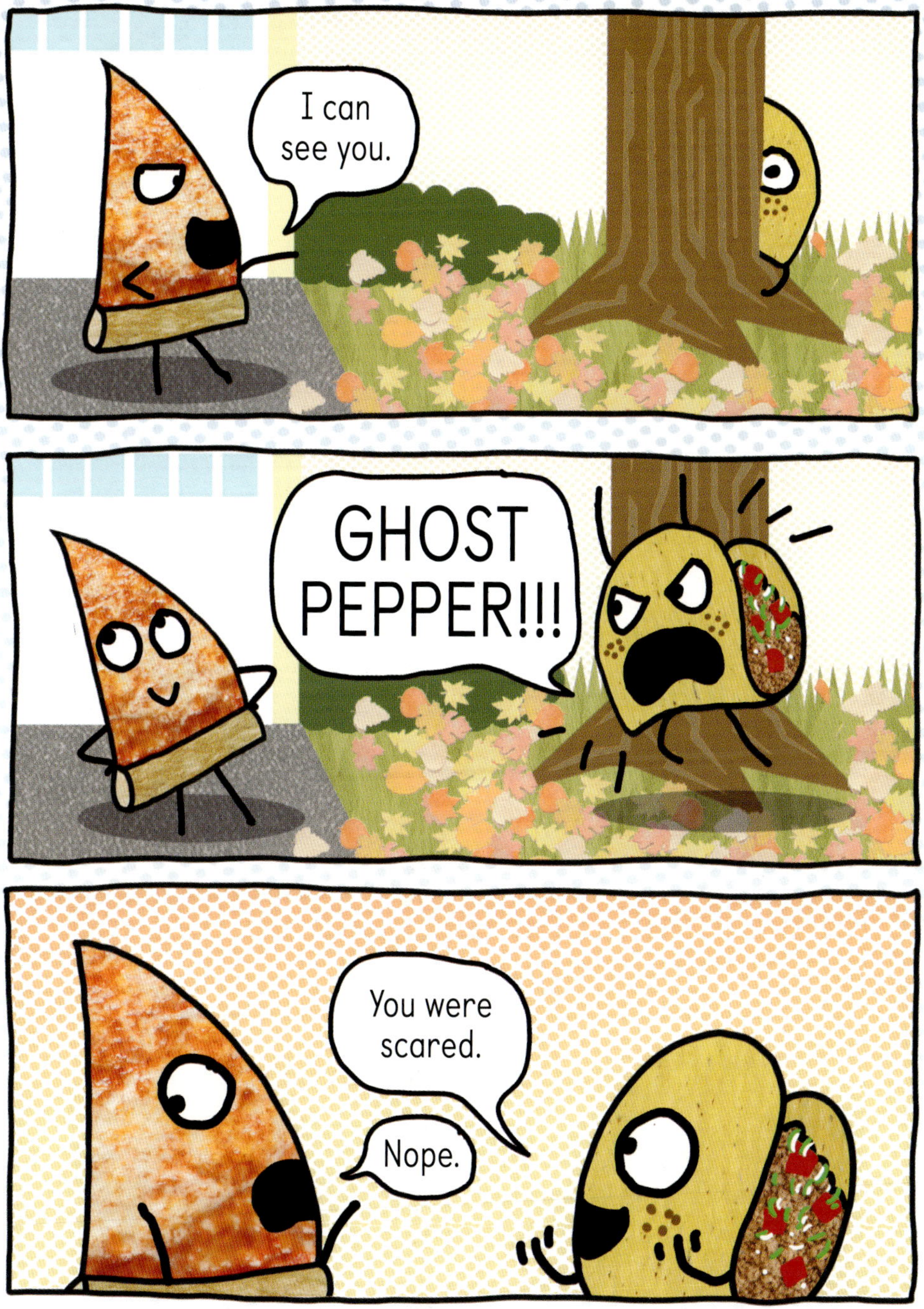
I can see you.
GHOST PEPPER!!!
You were scared.
Nope.

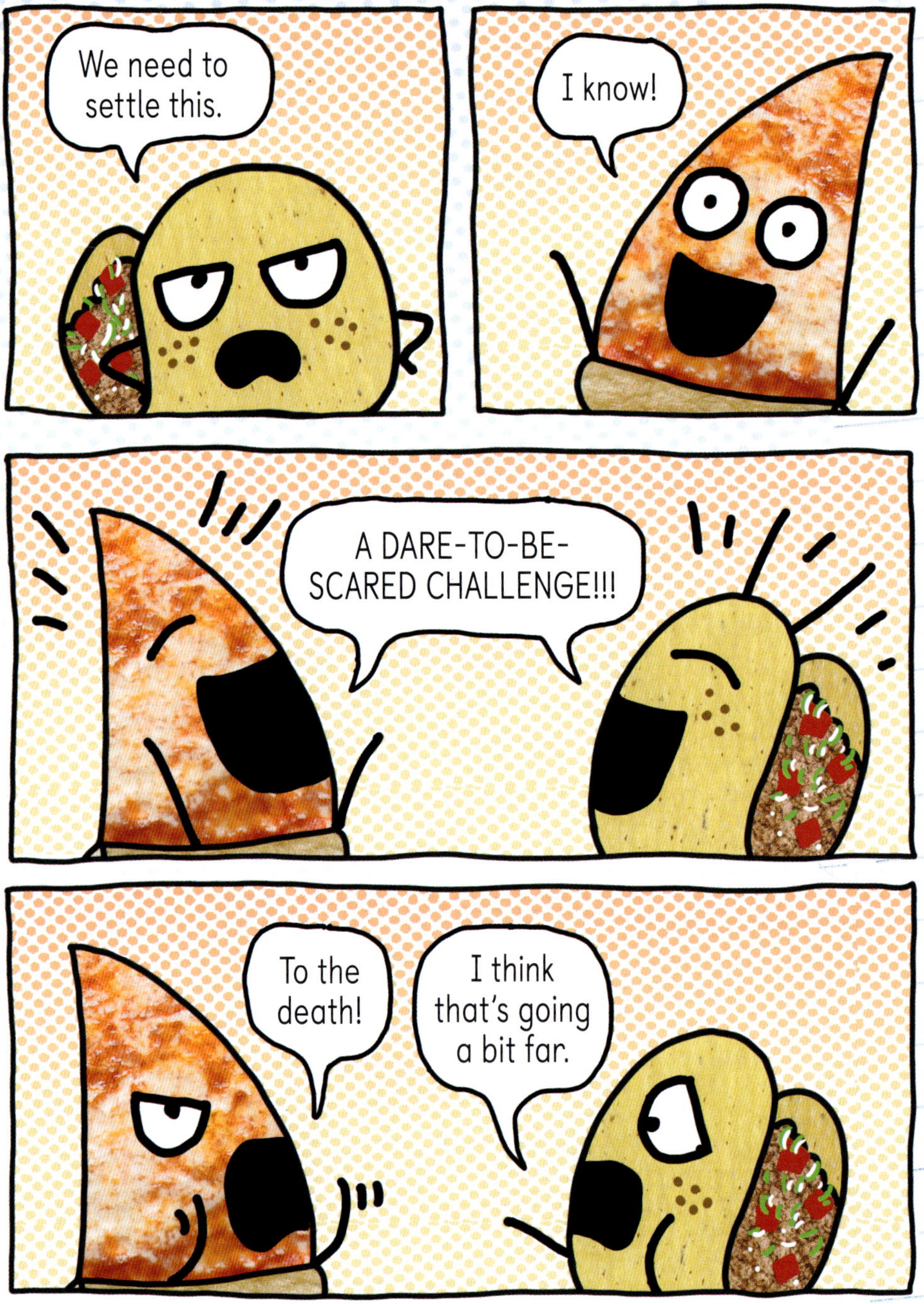
We need to settle this.
I know!
A DARE-TO-BE-SCARED CHALLENGE!!!
To the death!
I think that's going a bit far.

Chapter 2
Let the Challenge Begin

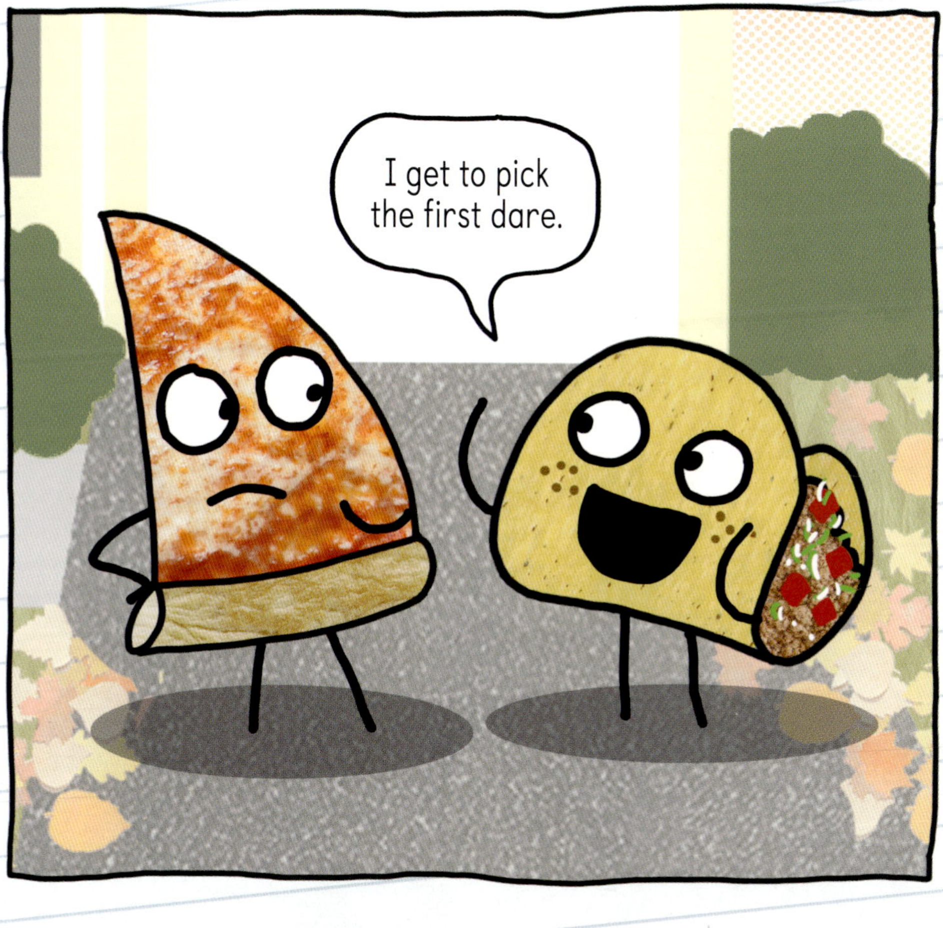
I get to pick the first dare.

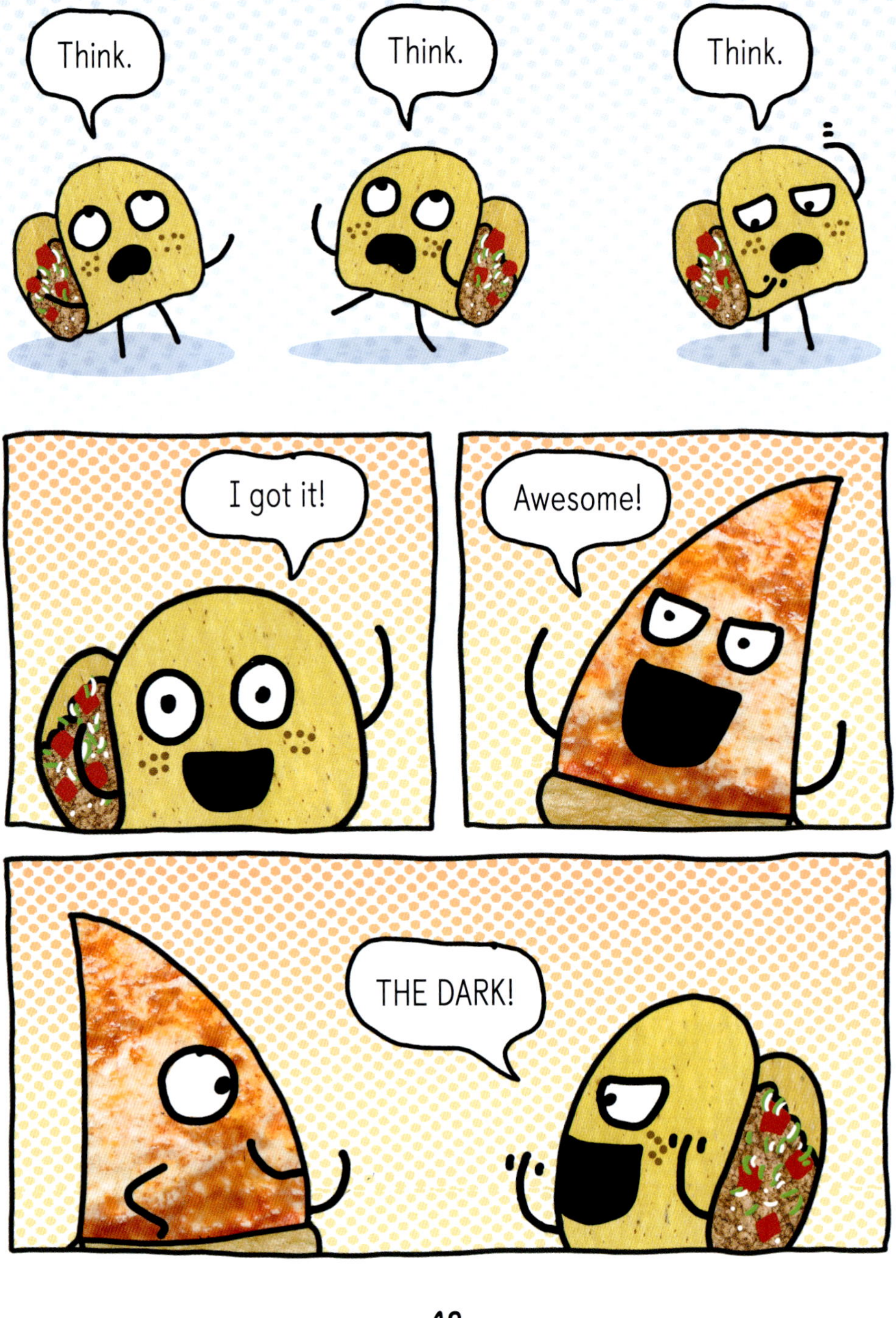
Think.
Think.
Think.
I got it!
Awesome!
THE DARK!

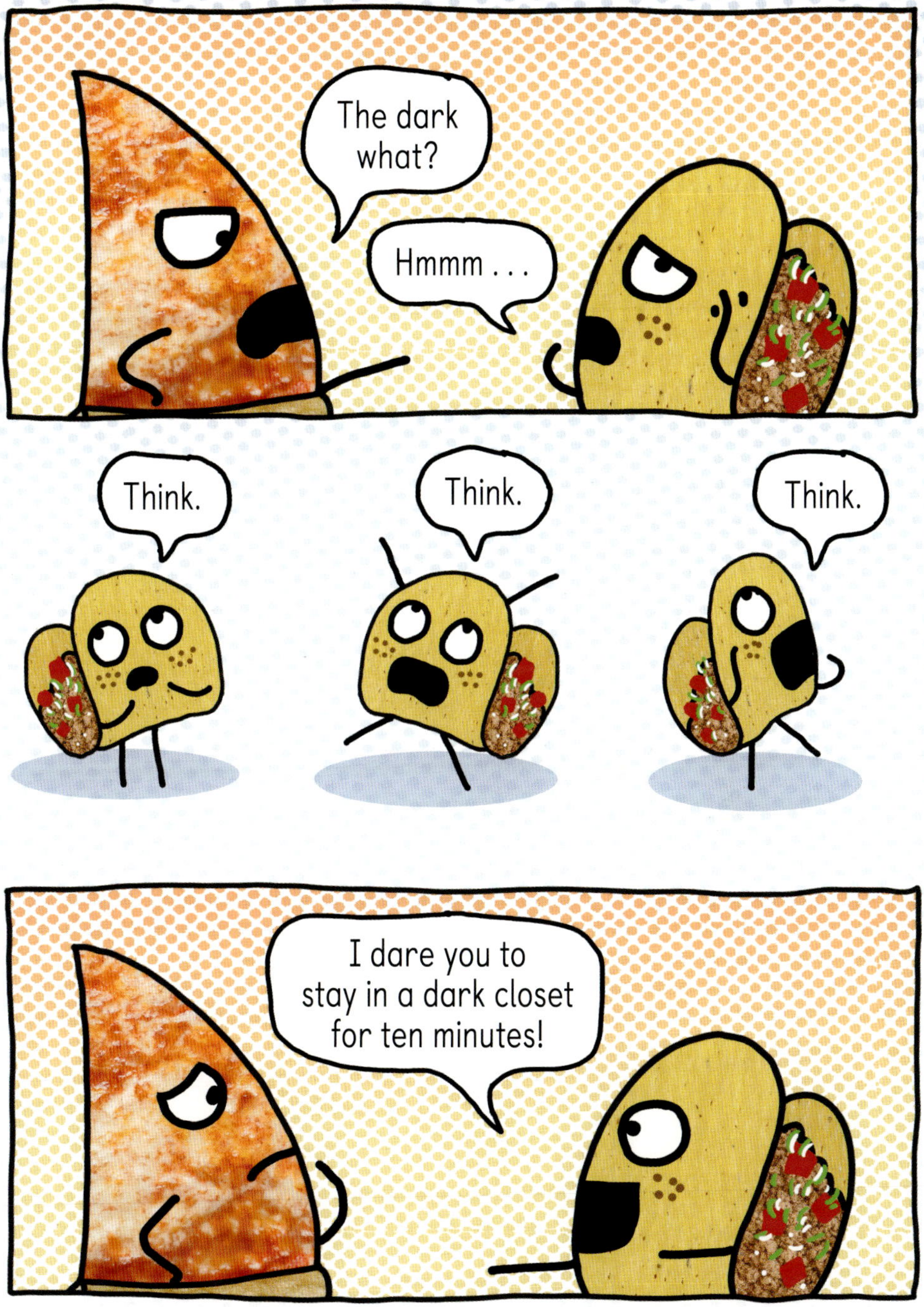
The dark what?
Hmmm . . .
Think.
Think.
Think.
I dare you to stay in a dark closet for ten minutes!

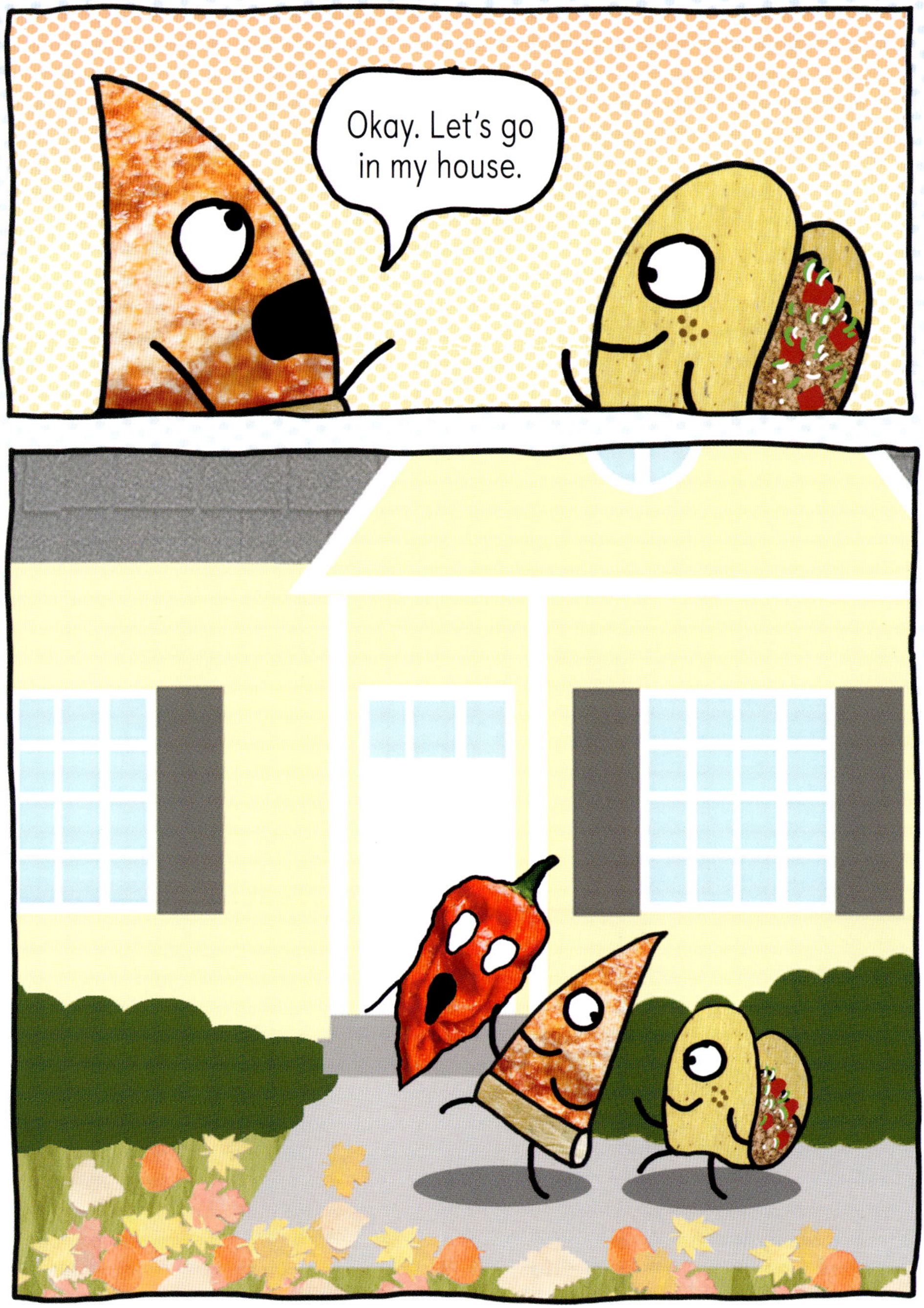
Okay. Let's go in my house.

I ♥ GOLF
#1 mom

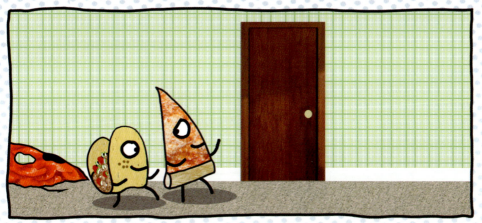

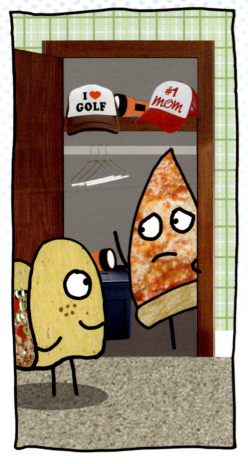

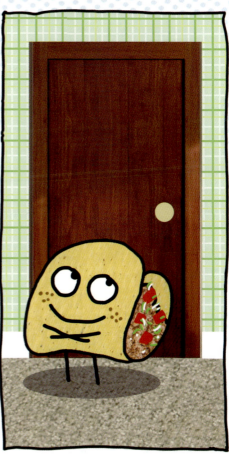

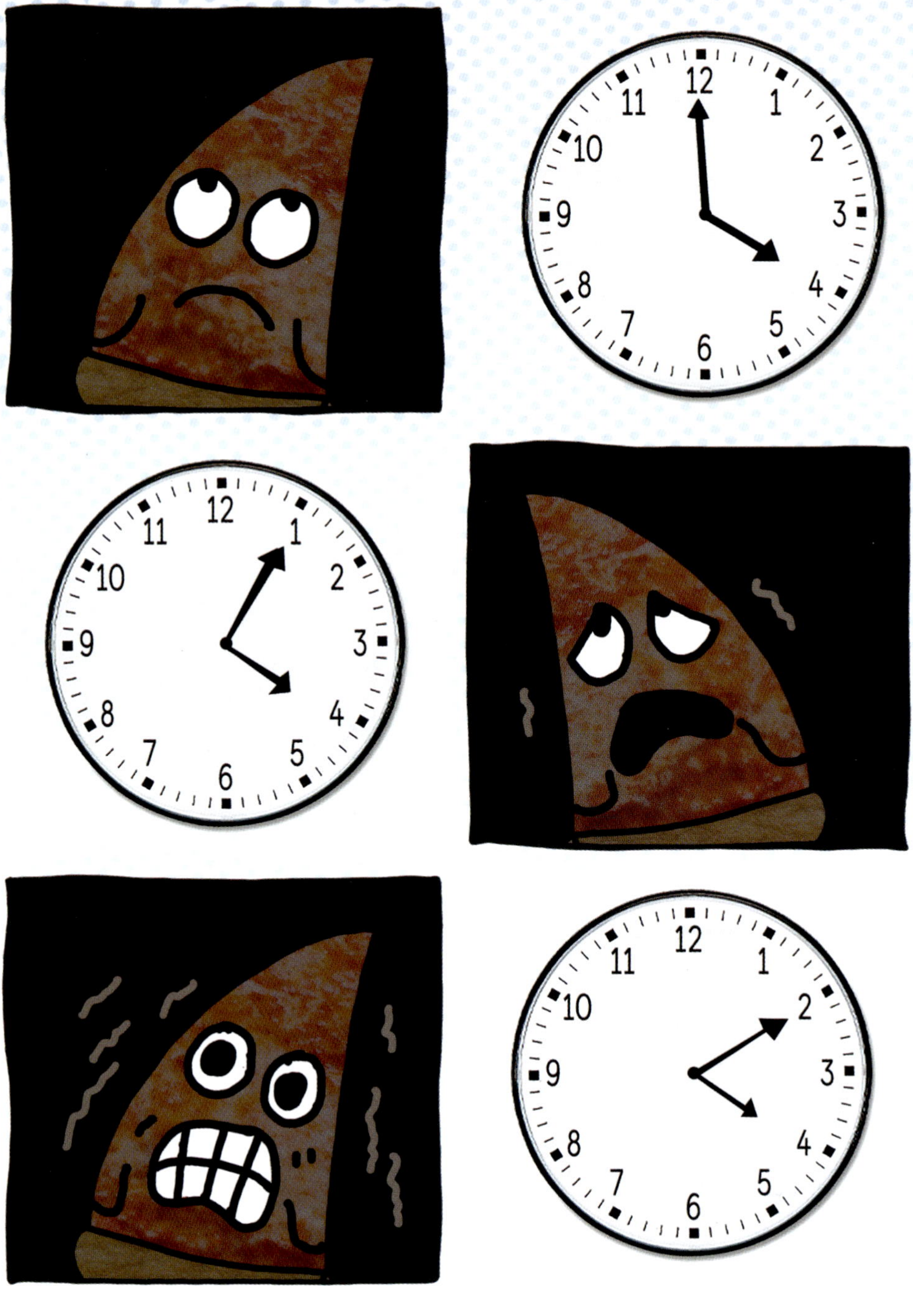

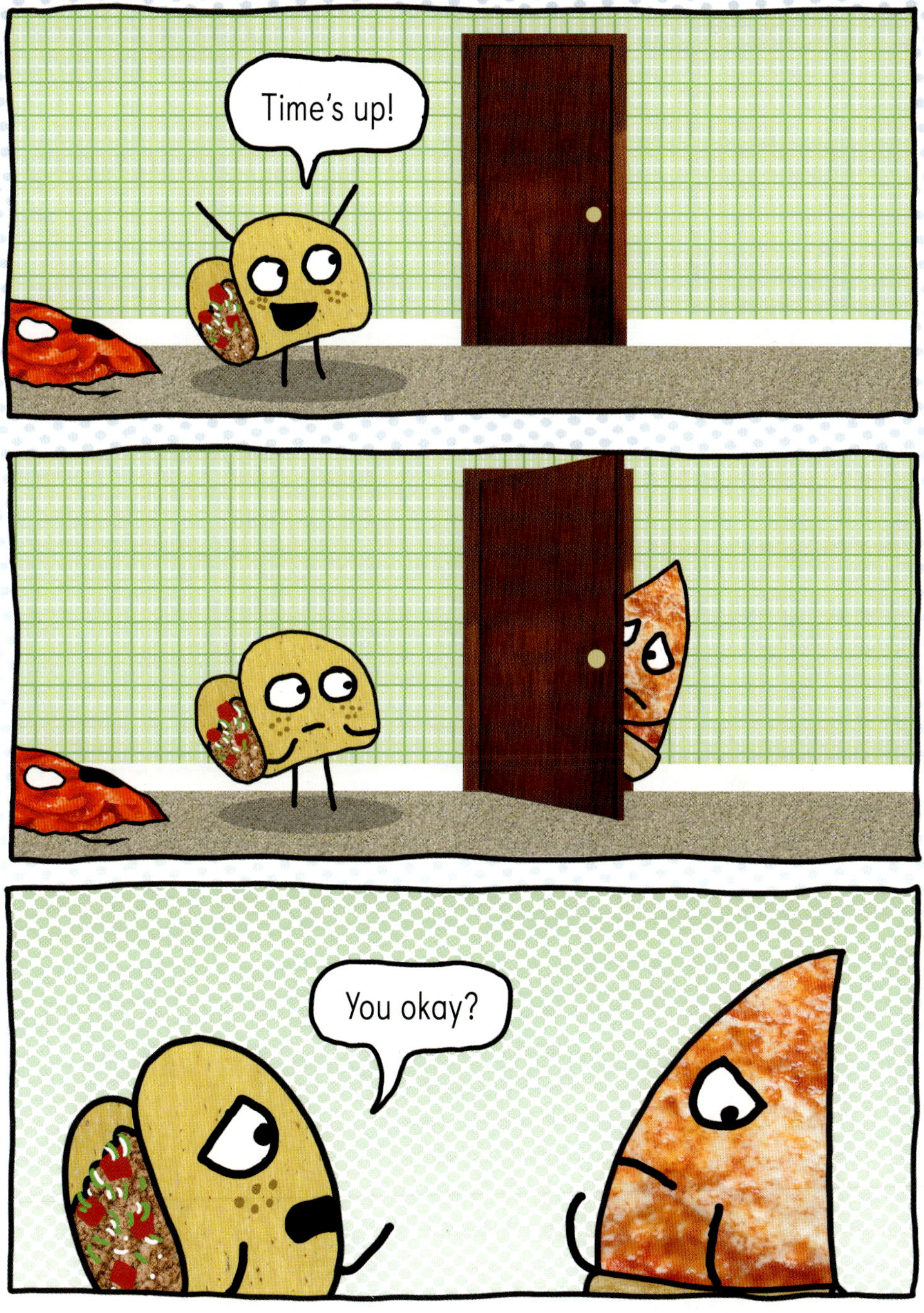
Time's up!
You okay?

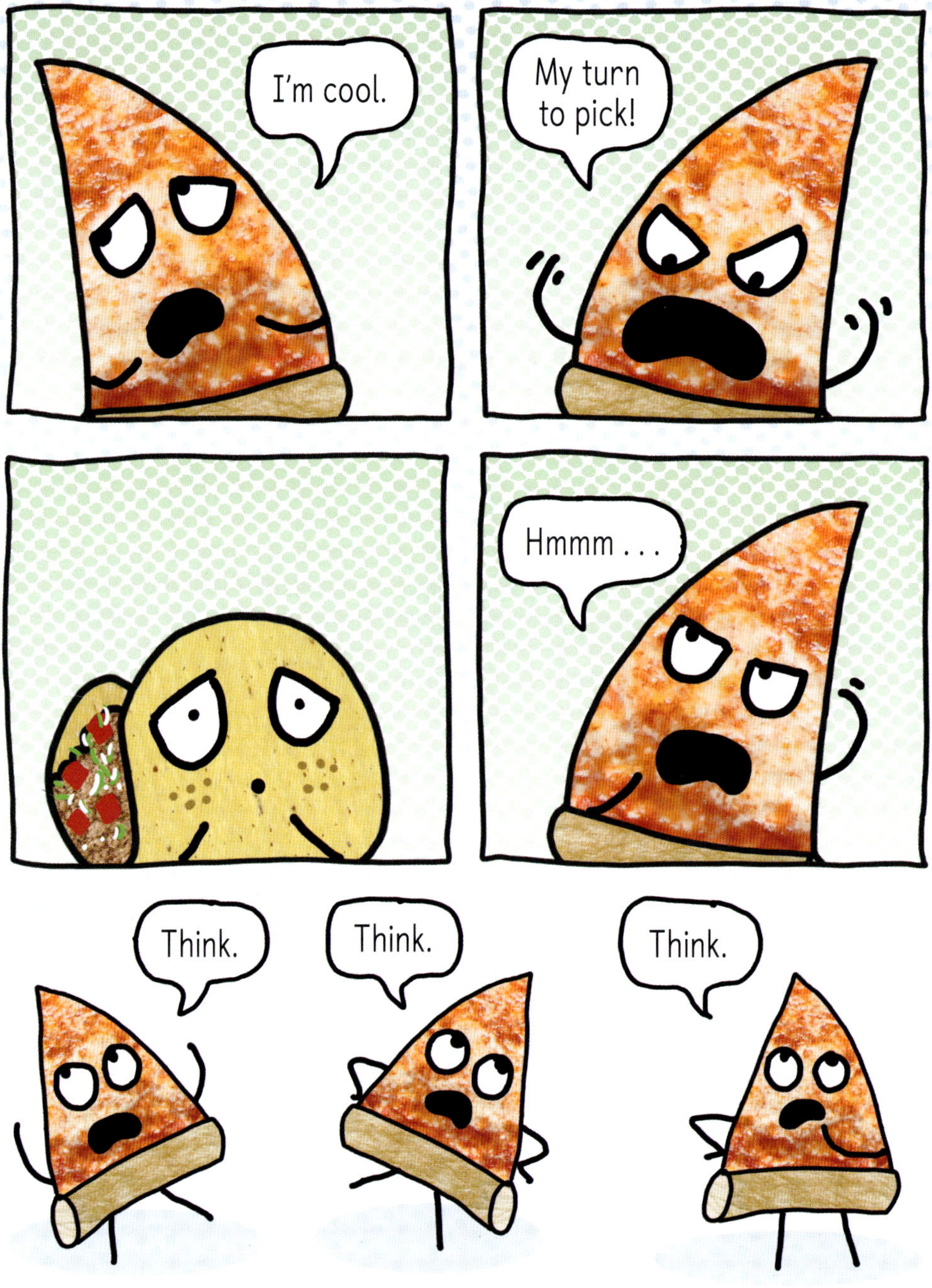
I'm cool.
My turn to pick!
Hmmm . . .
Think.
Think.
Think.

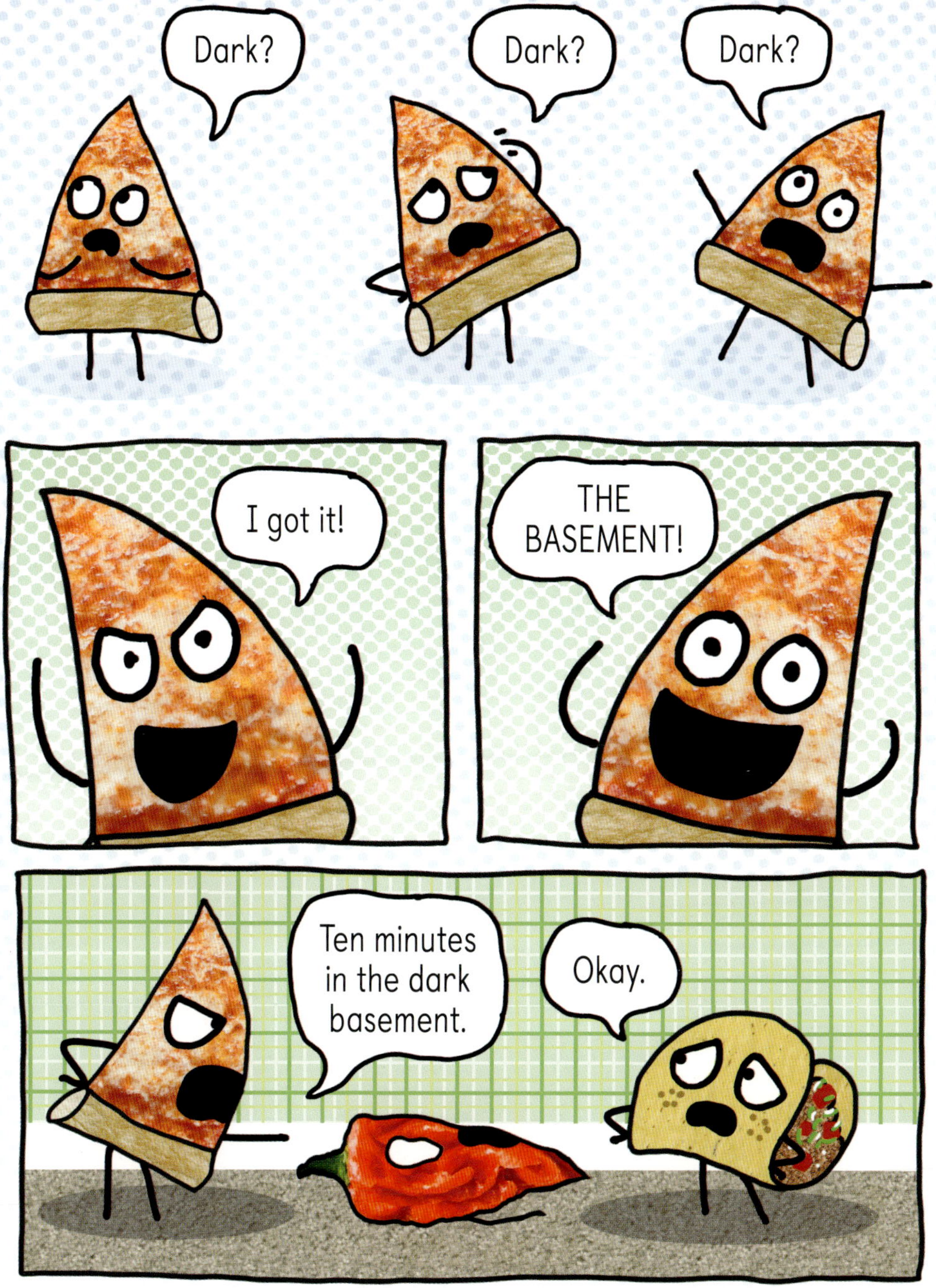
Dark?
Dark?
Dark?
I got it!
THE BASEMENT!
Ten minutes in the dark basement.
Okay.

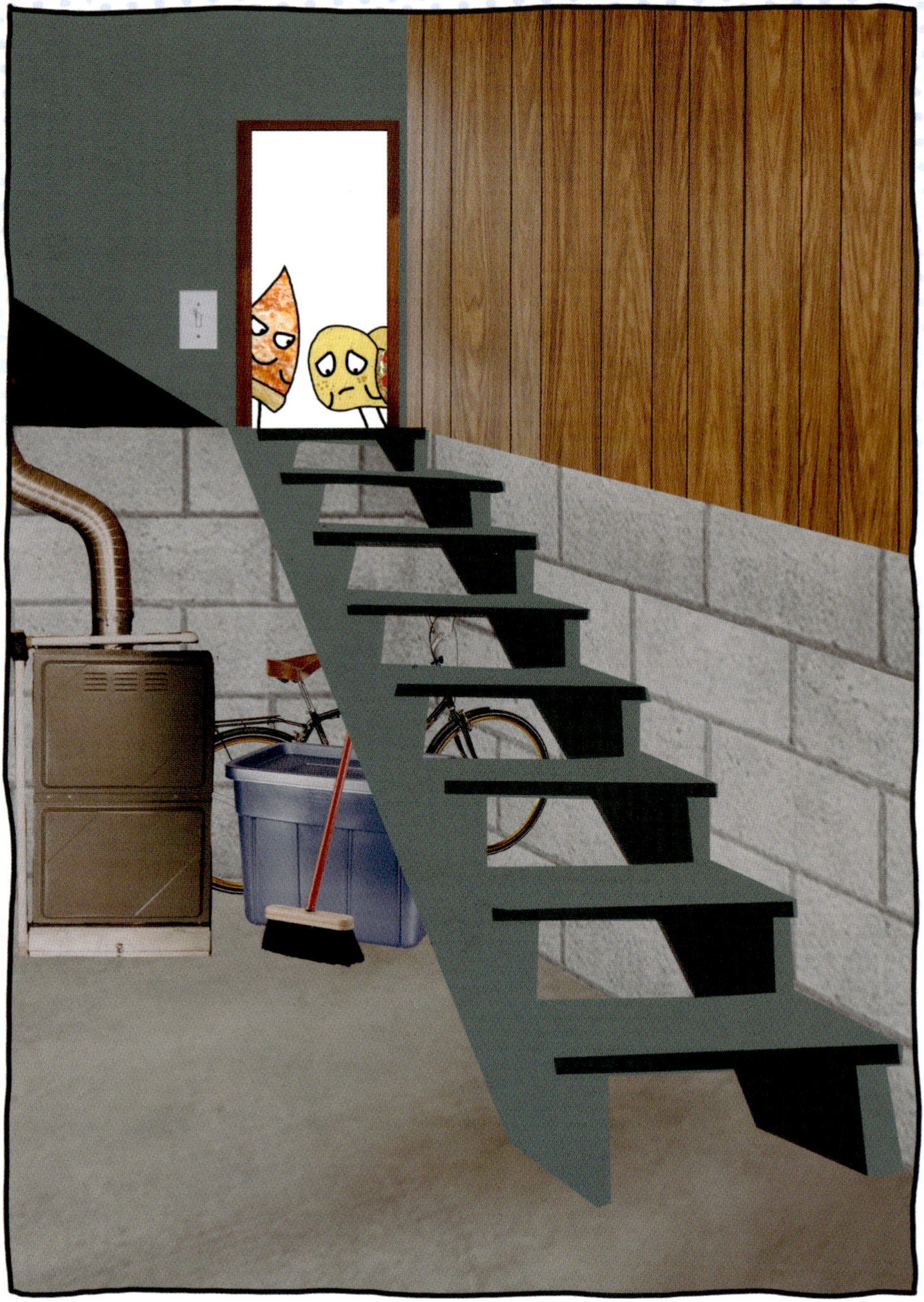

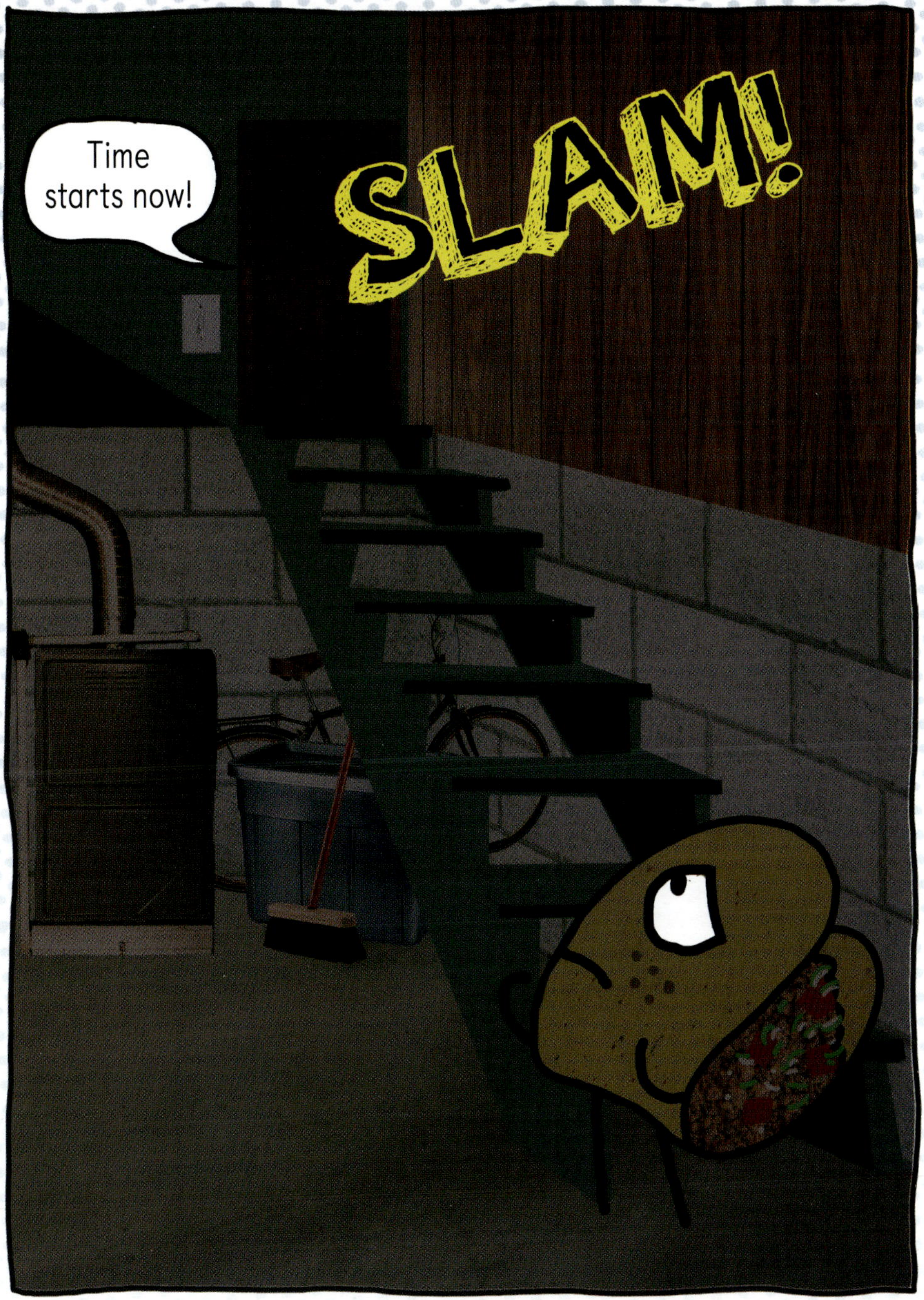
Time starts now!
SLAM!

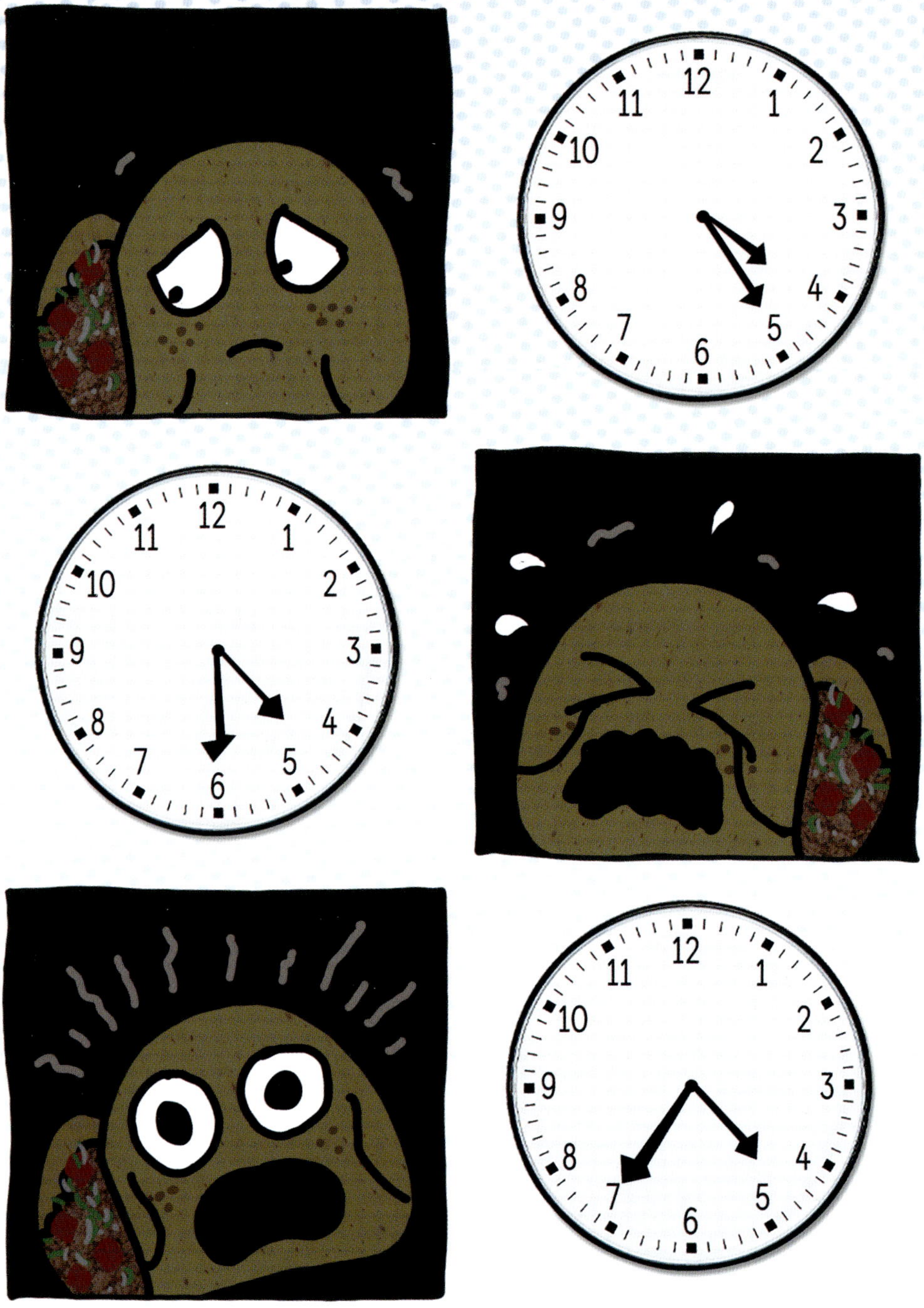

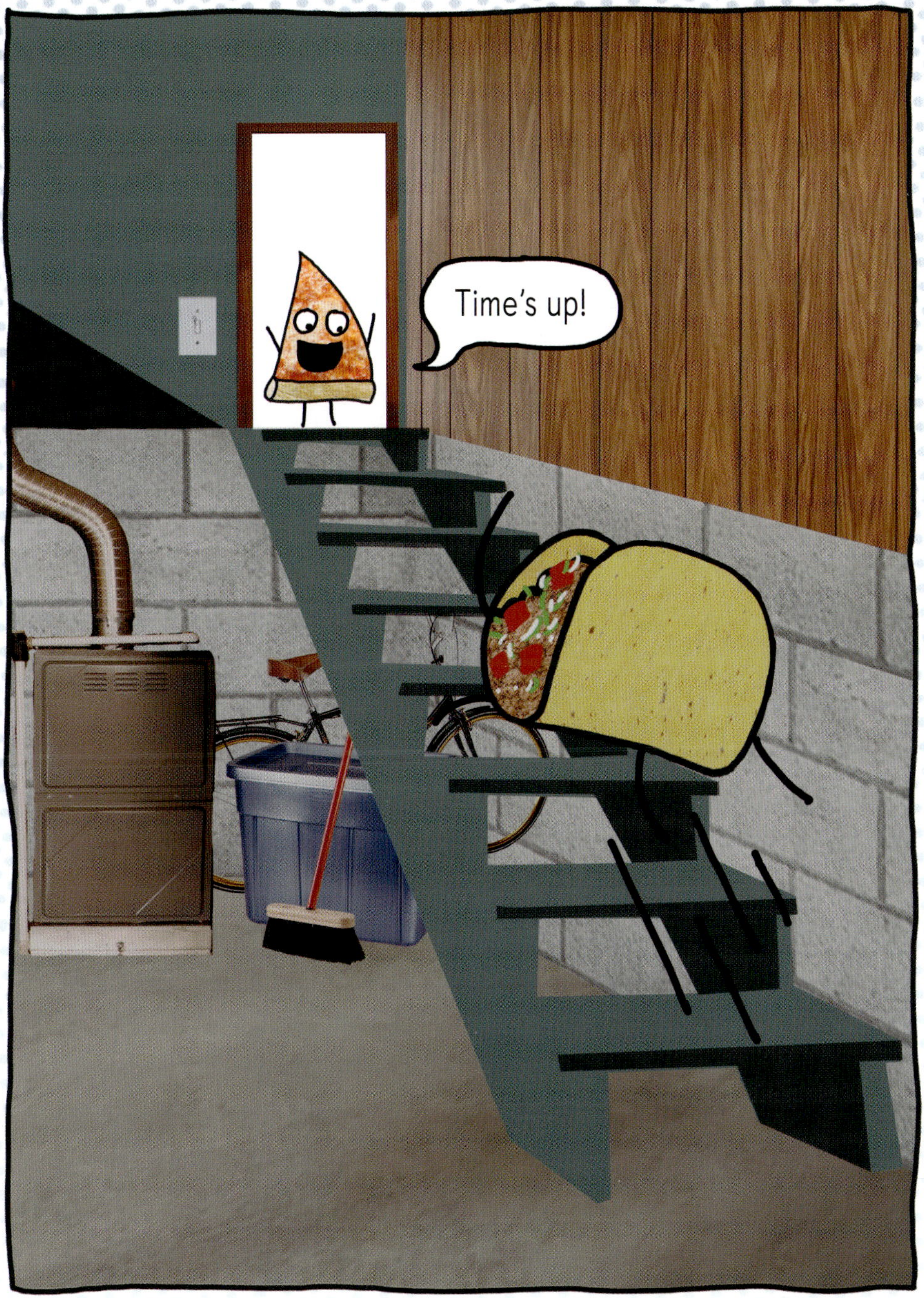
Time's up!

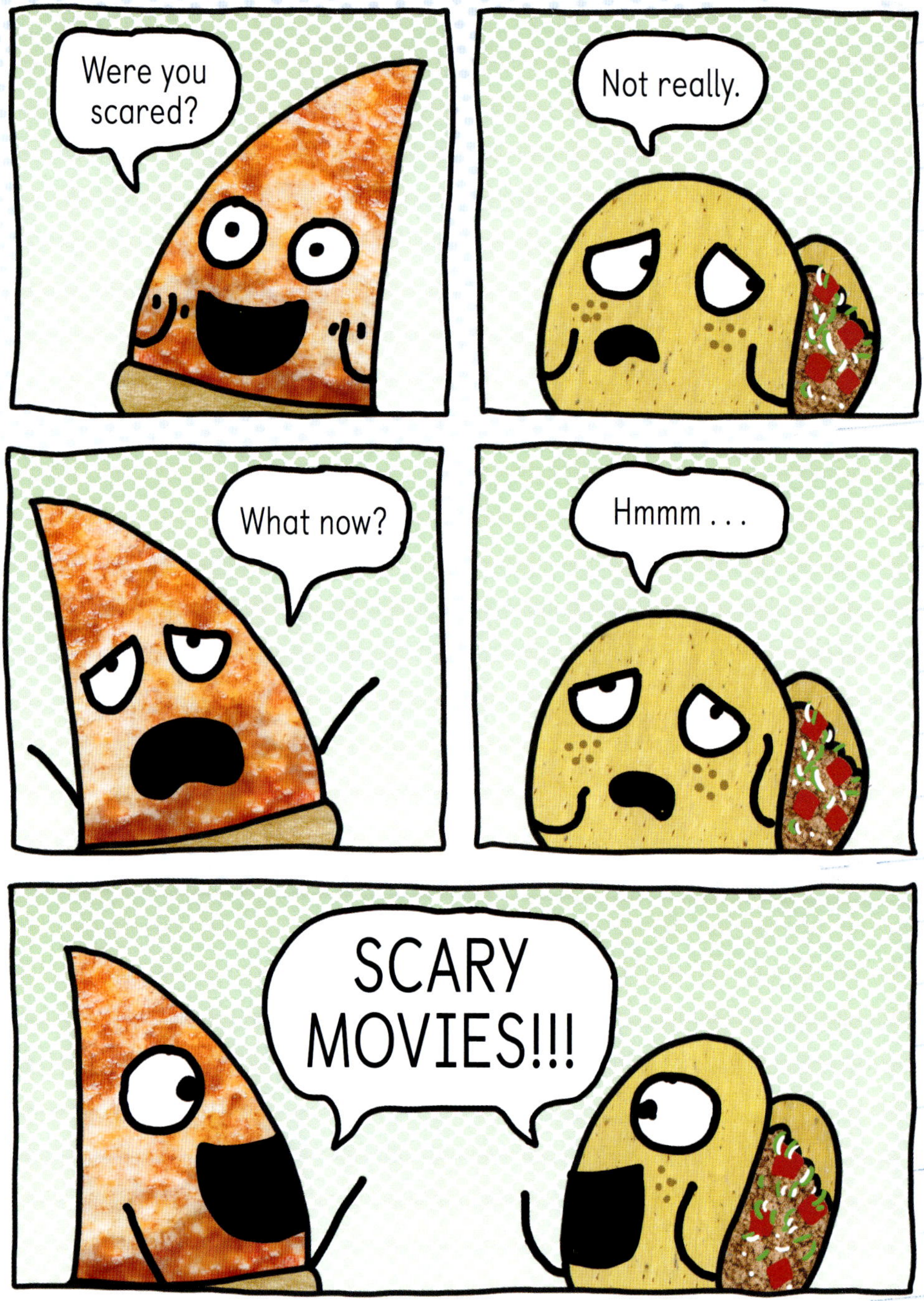
Were you scared?
Not really.
What now?
Hmmm . . .
SCARY MOVIES!!!

Chapter 3
Scariest Dariest Movie!

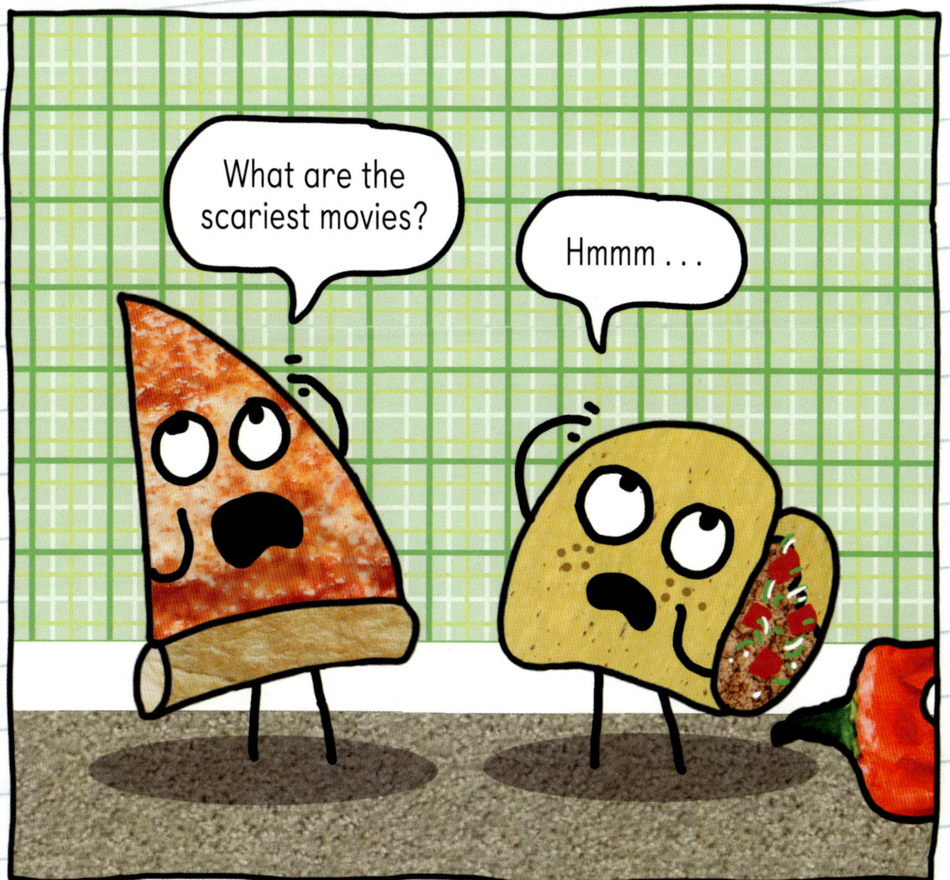
What are the scariest movies?
Hmmm . . .

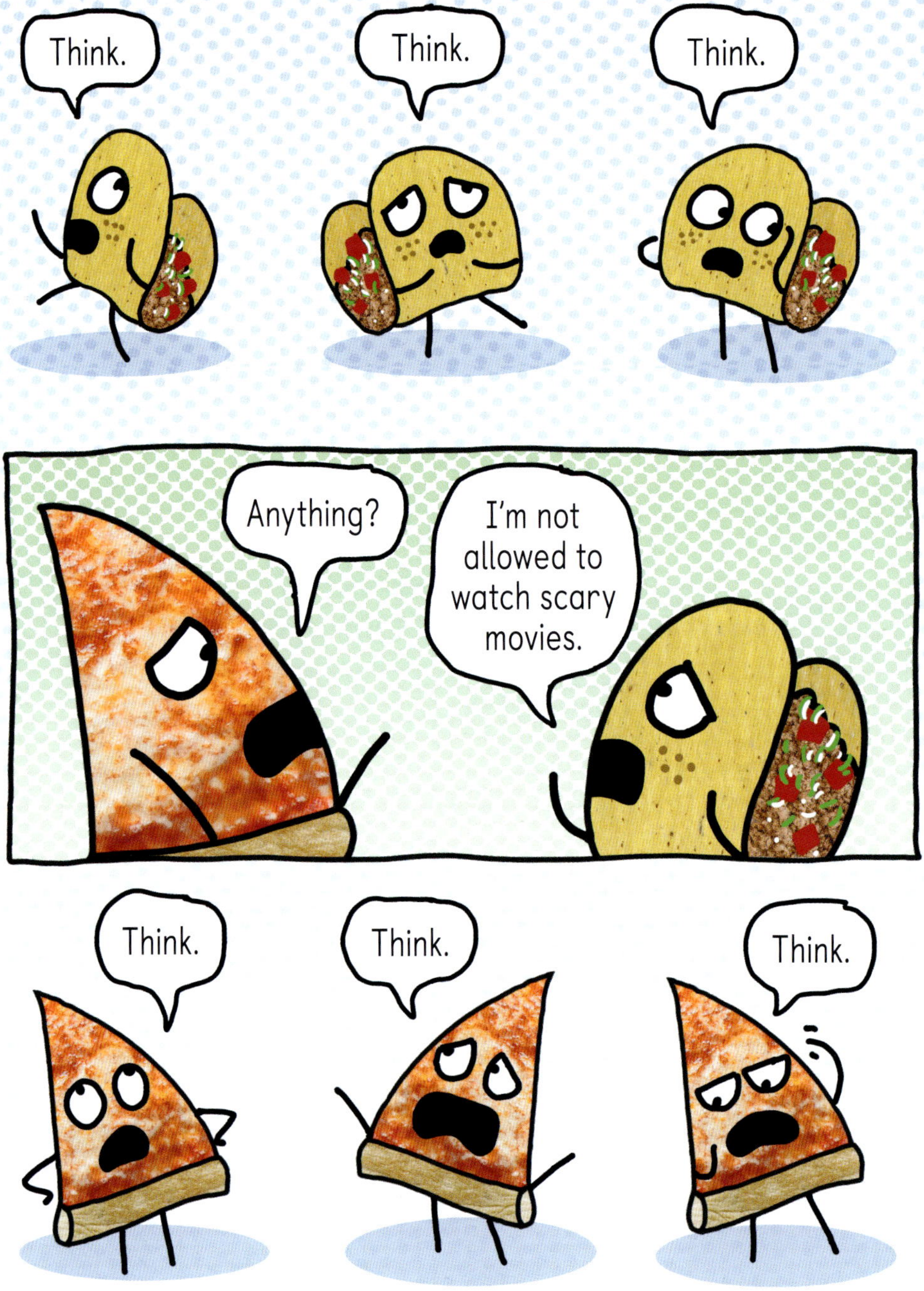
Think.
Think.
Think.
Anything?
I'm not allowed to watch scary movies.
Think.
Think.
Think.

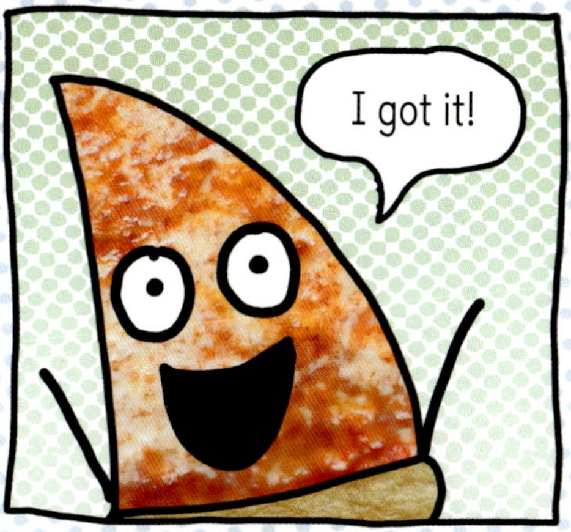
I got it!

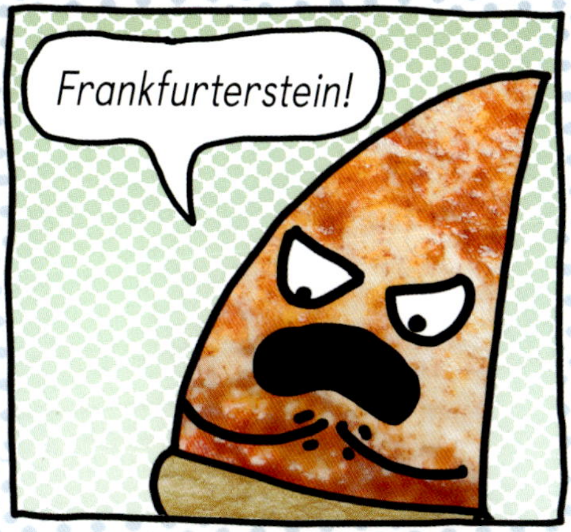
Frankfurterstein!

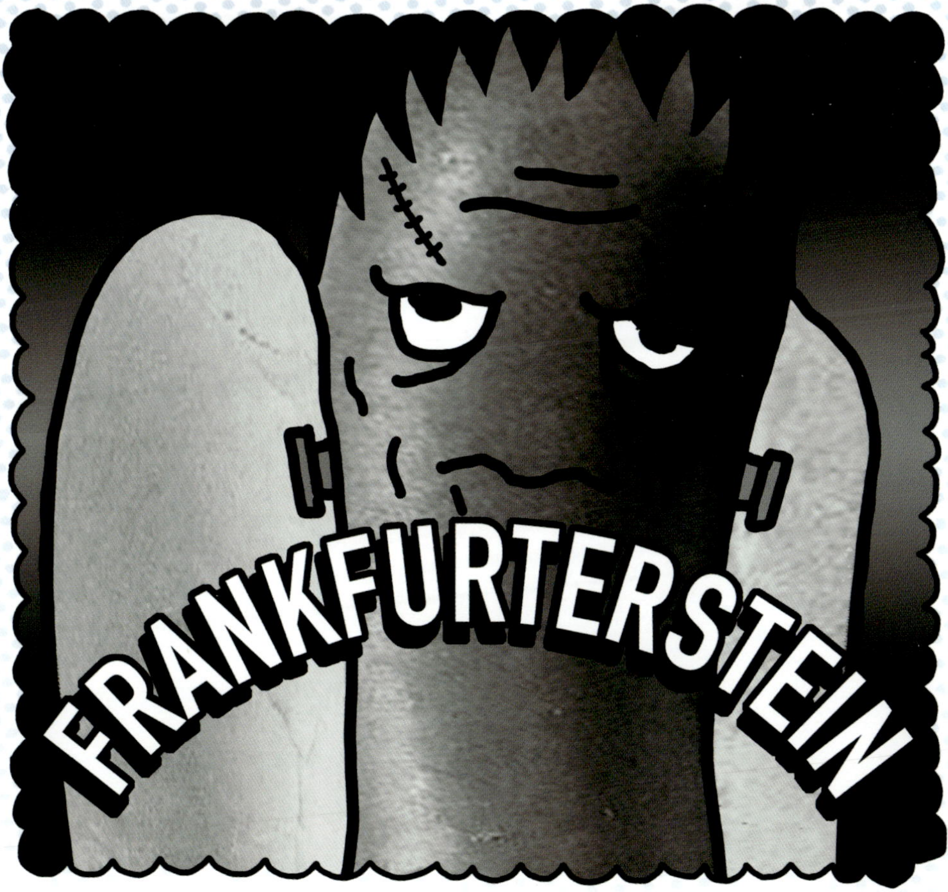
FRANKFURTERSTEIN

YAAAS!

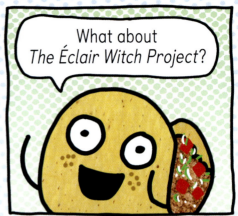

What about *The Éclair Witch Project*?

THE ÉCLAIR WITCH PROJECT

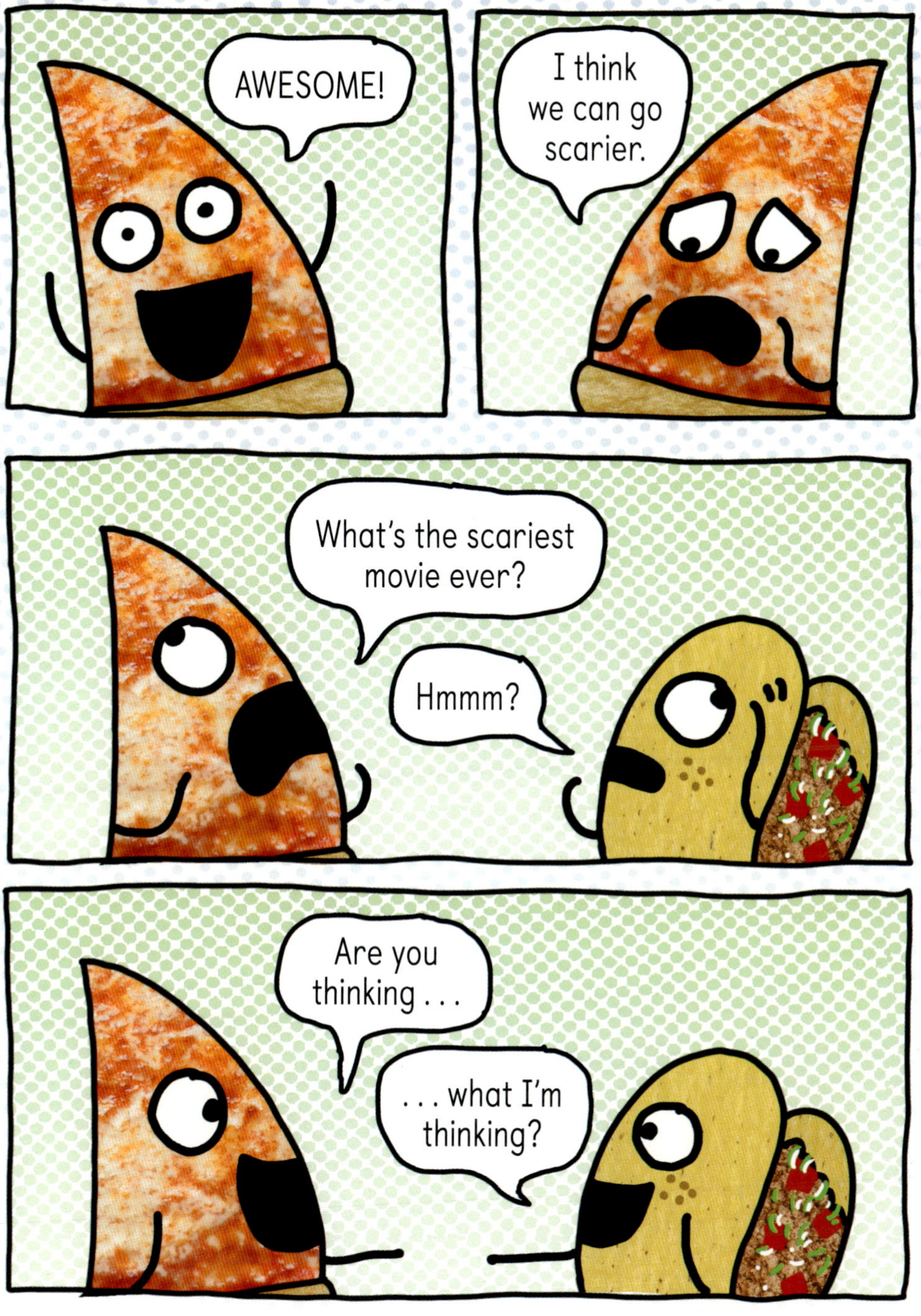
AWESOME!
I think we can go scarier.
What's the scariest movie ever?
Hmmm?
Are you thinking . . .
. . . what I'm thinking?

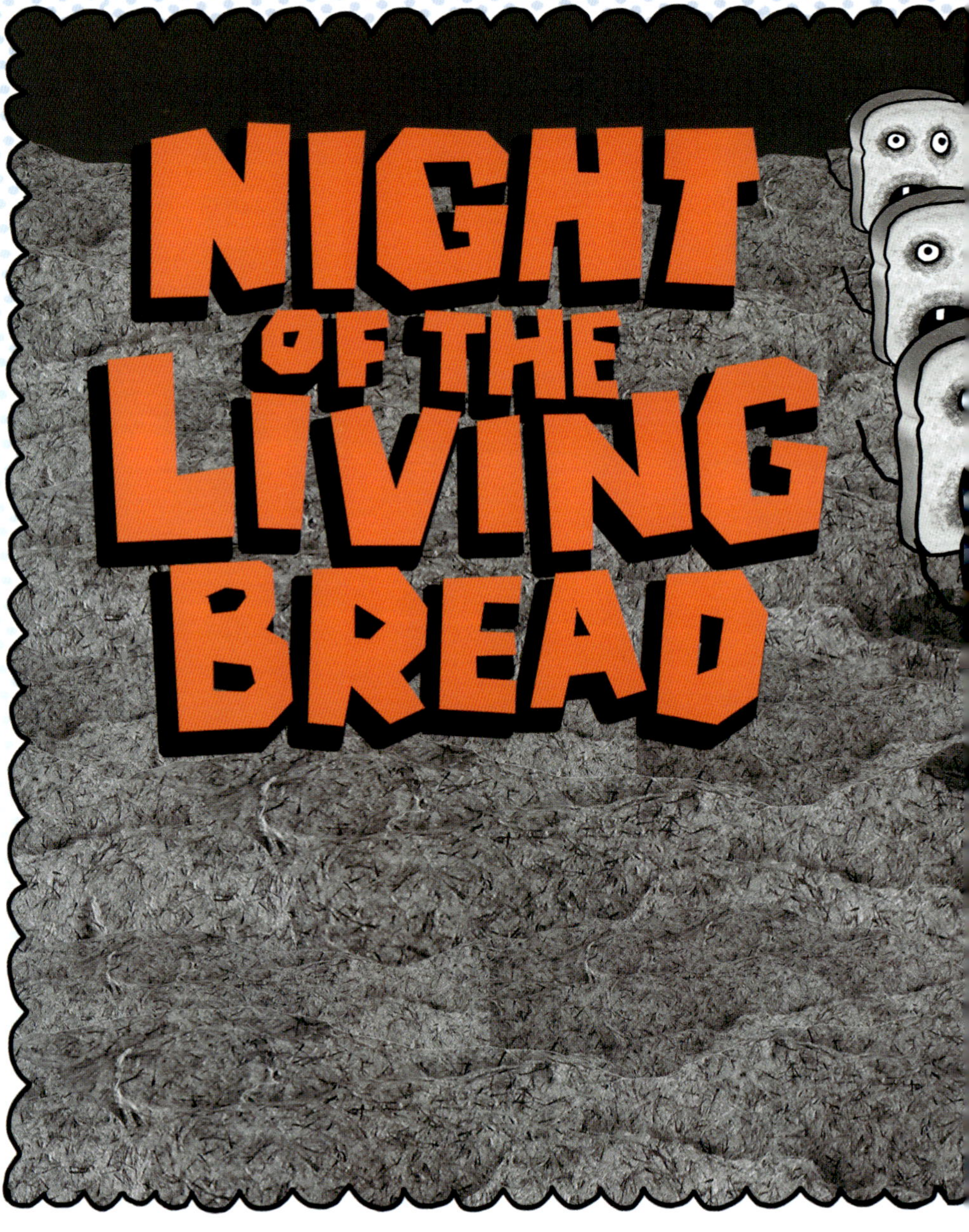
NIGHT
OF THE
LIVING
BREAD

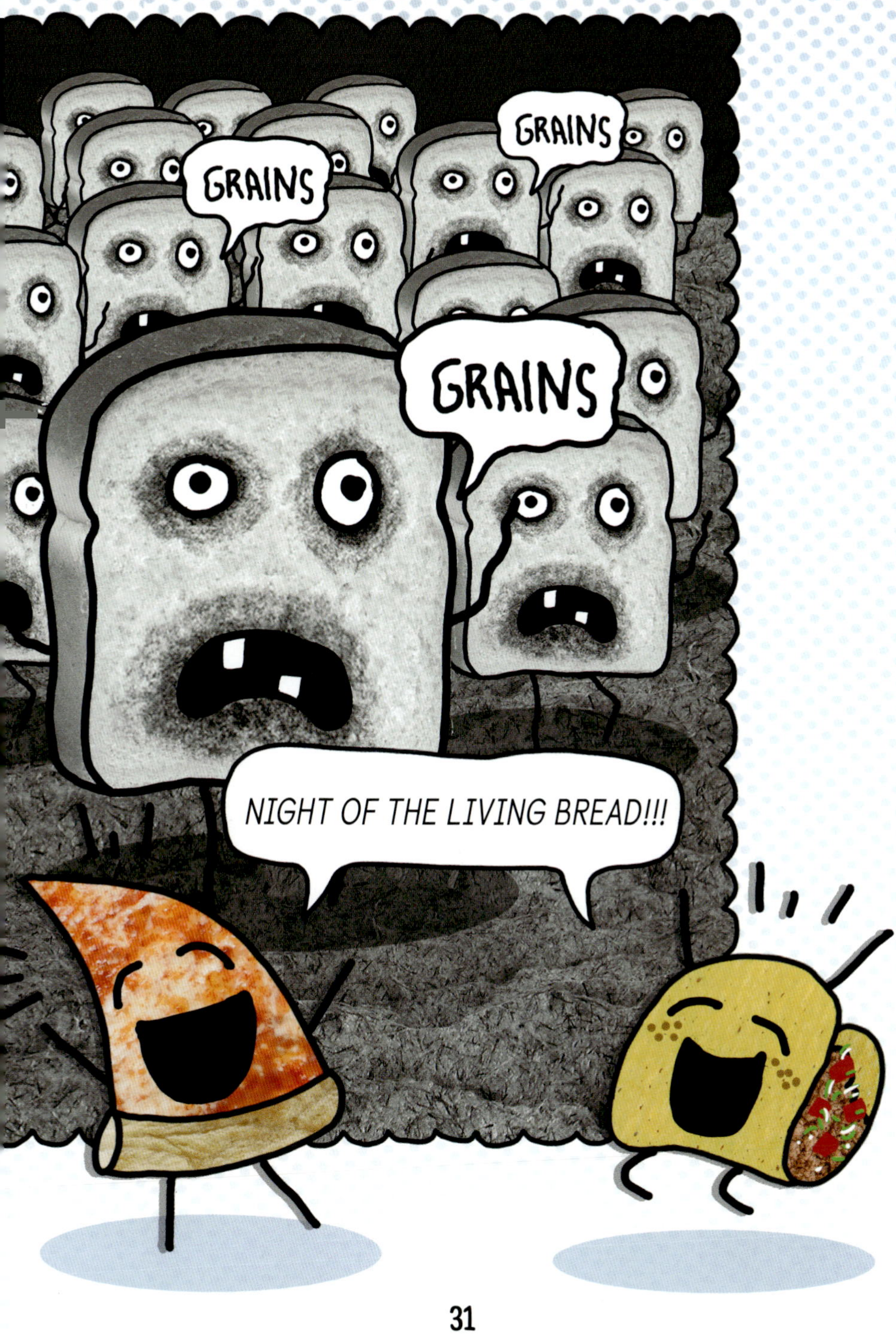
GRAINS
GRAINS
GRAINS
NIGHT OF THE LIVING BREAD!!!

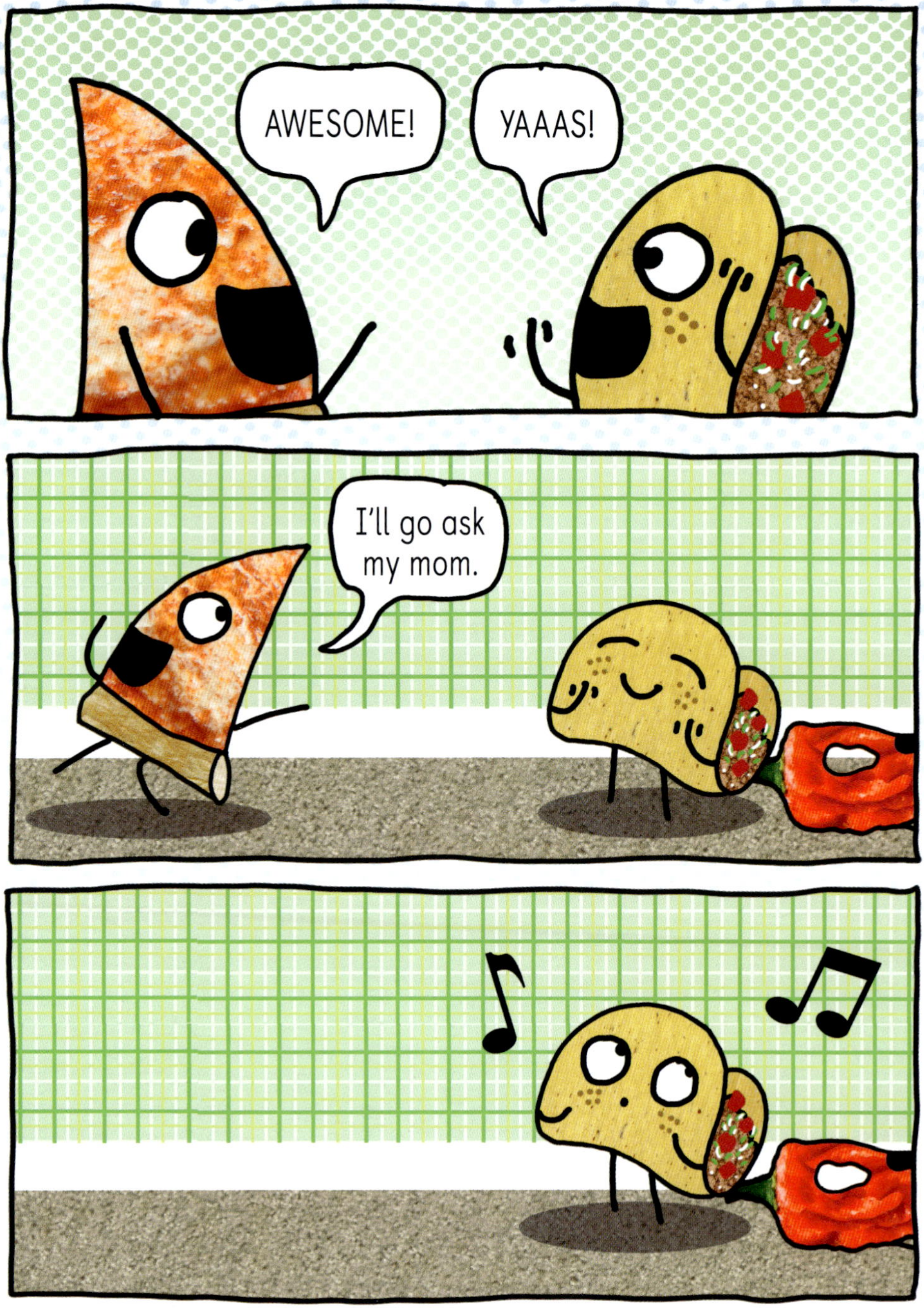
AWESOME!
YAAAS!
I'll go ask my mom.

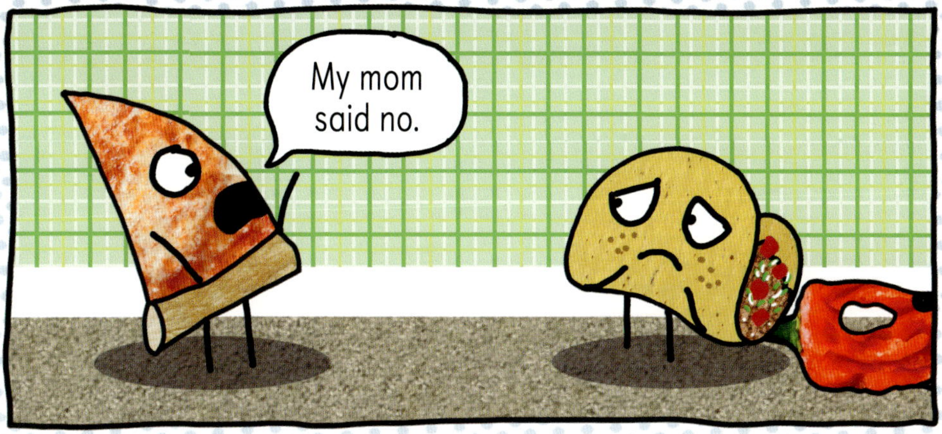
My mom said no.

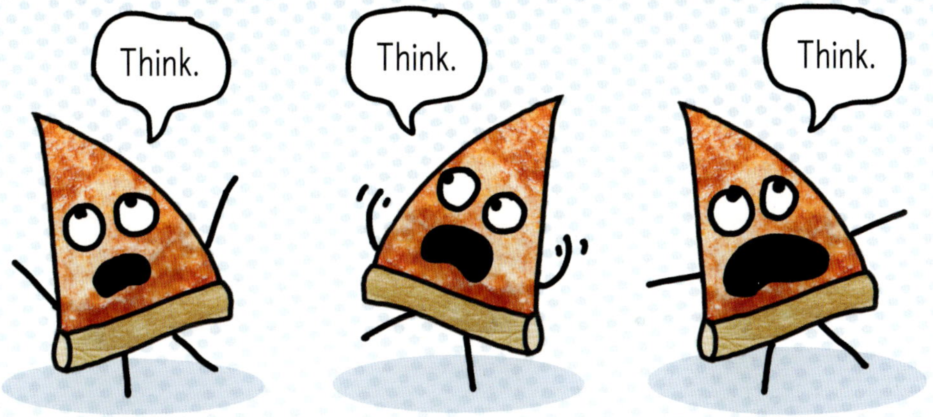
Think.
Think.
Think.

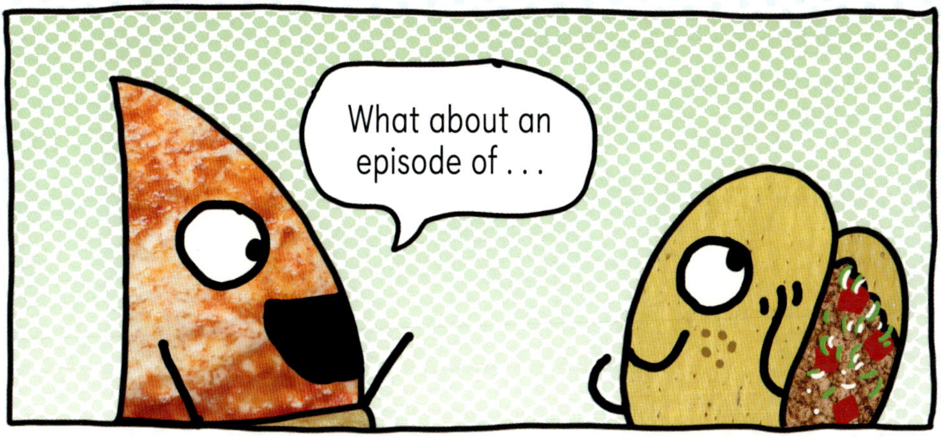
What about an episode of . . .

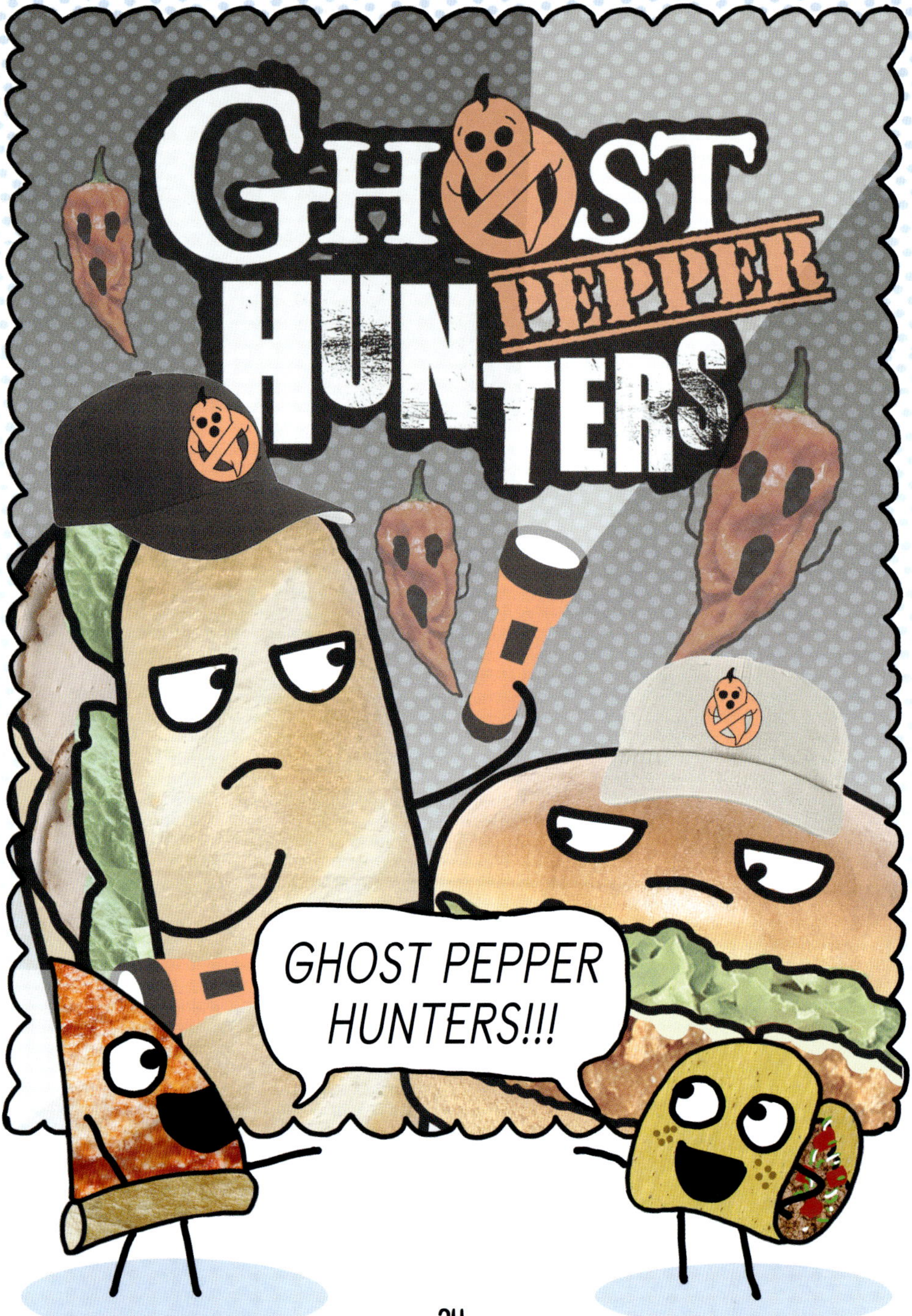
GHOST PEPPER HUNTERS
GHOST PEPPER HUNTERS!!!

I'll go ask my mom.
SHE SAID YES!
YAAAS!

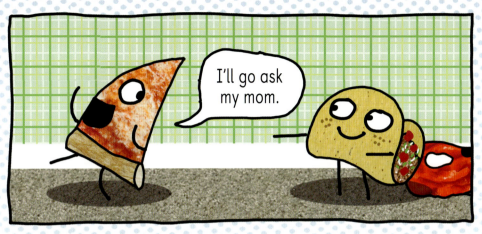

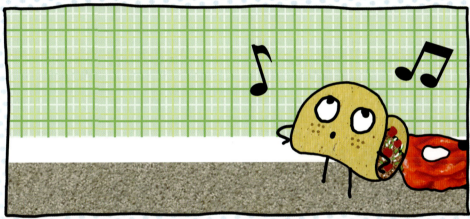

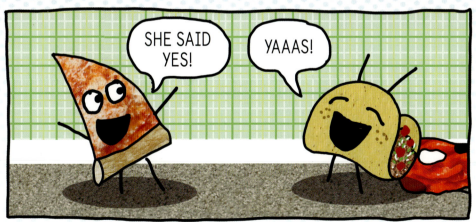

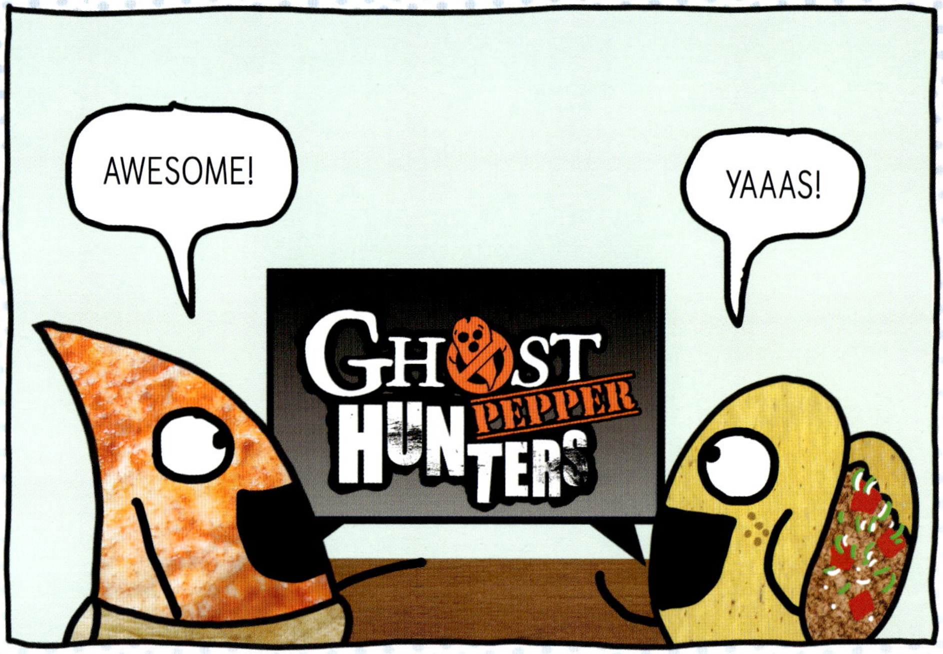
AWESOME!
YAAAS!
GHOST PEPPER HUNTERS

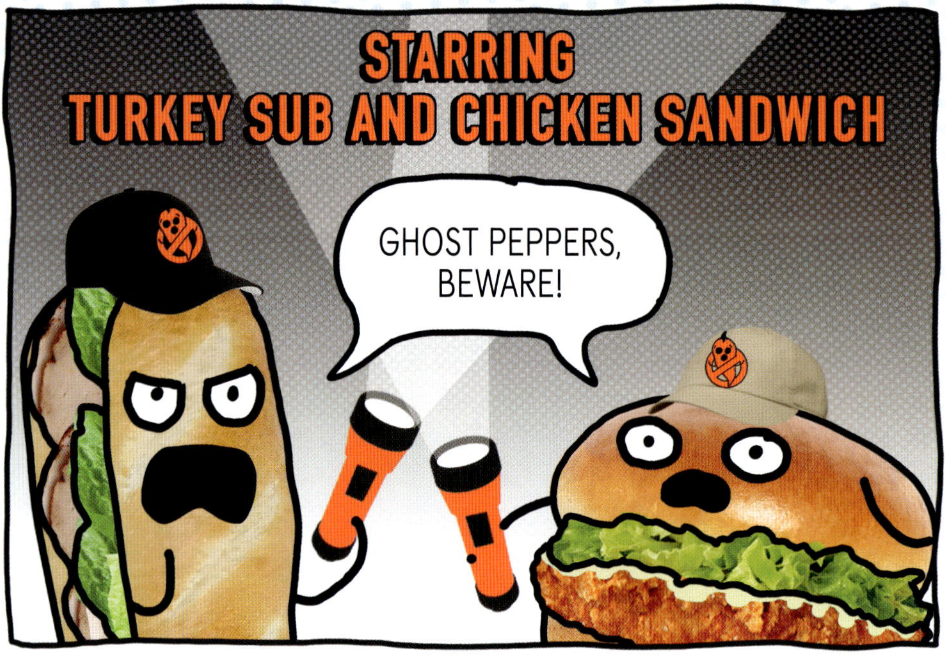
STARRING
TURKEY SUB AND CHICKEN SANDWICH
GHOST PEPPERS, BEWARE!

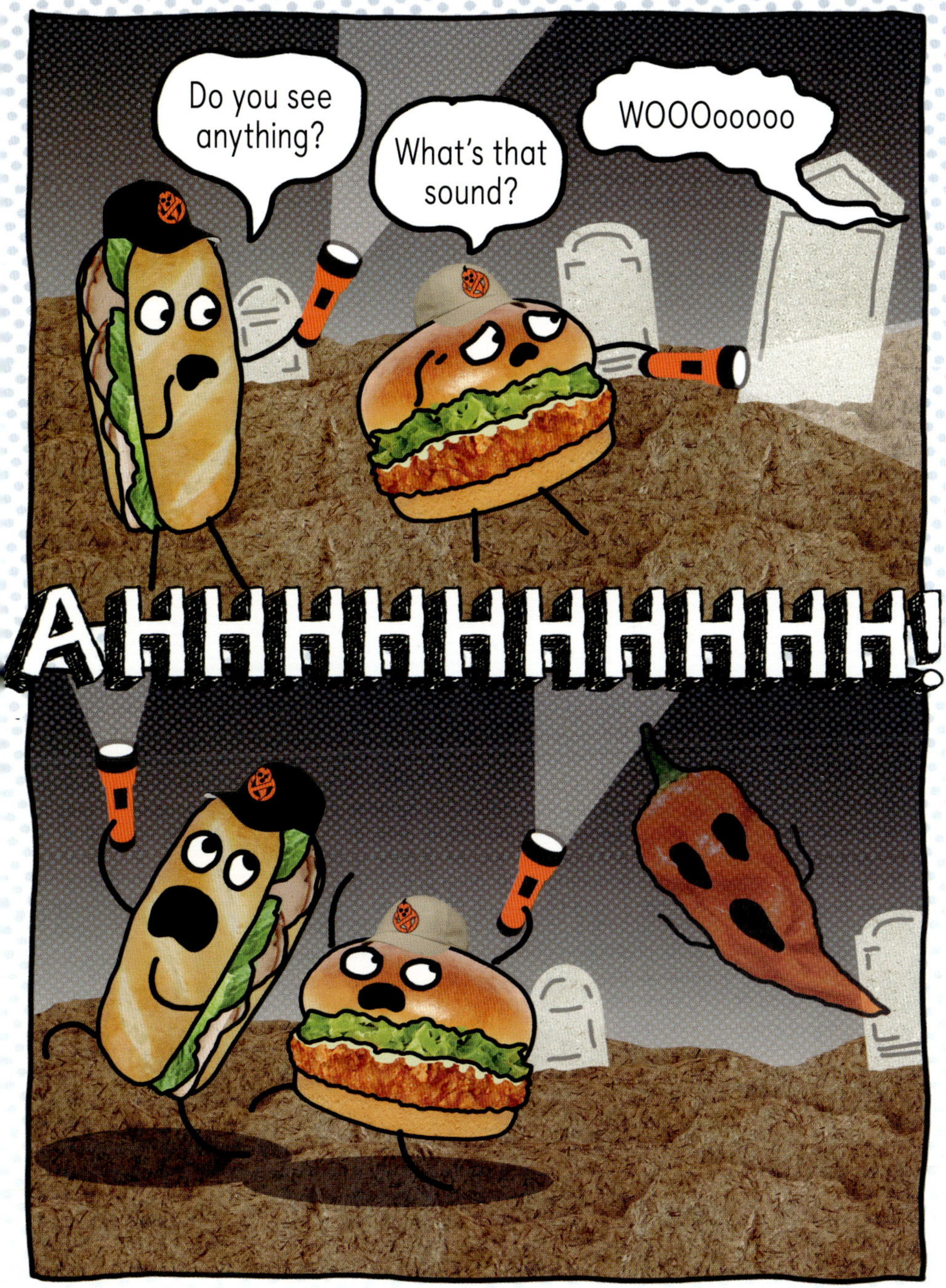
Do you see anything?
What's that sound?
WOOOooooo
AHHHHHHHHHHHH!

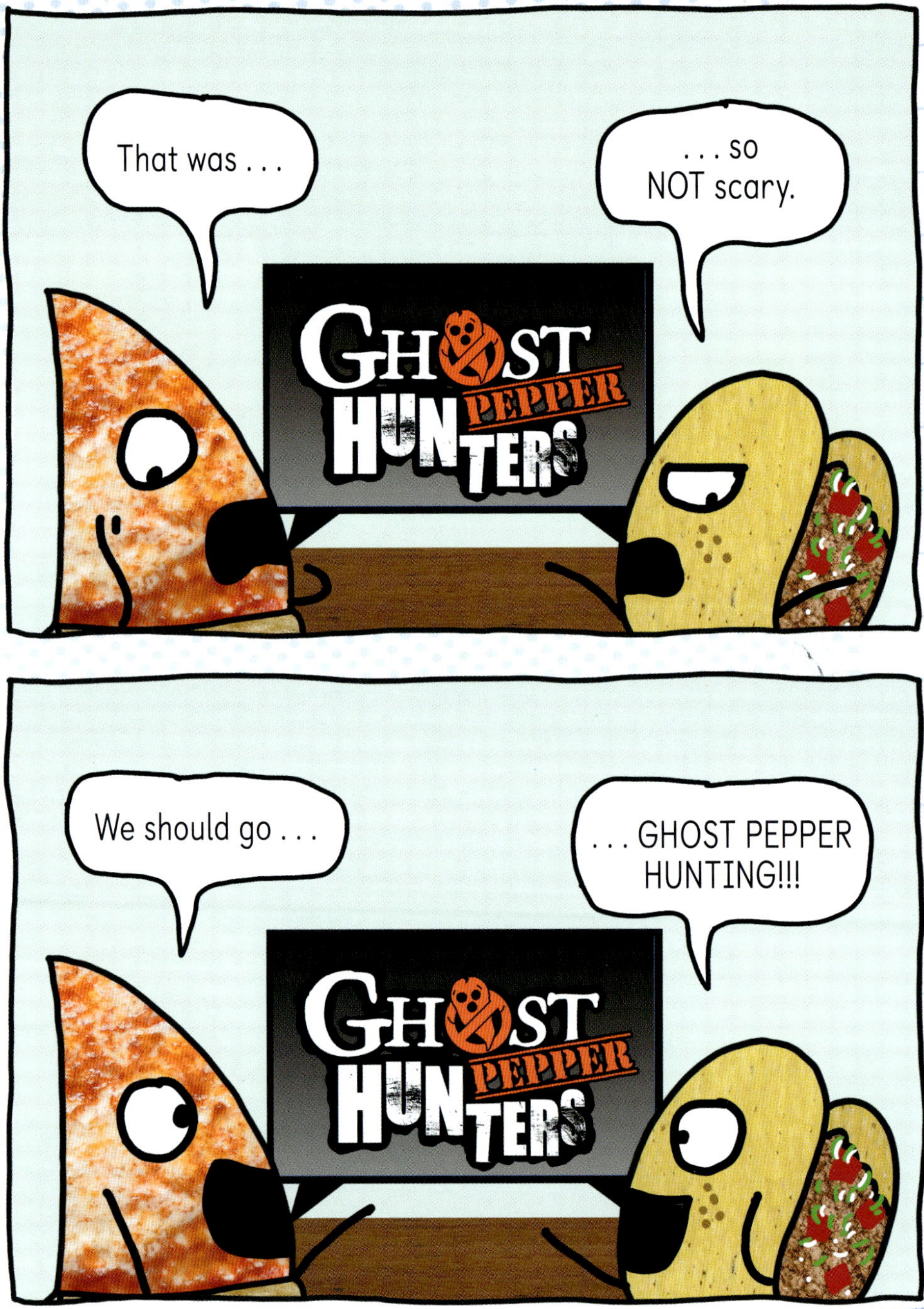
That was . . .
. . . so NOT scary.
GHOST PEPPER HUNTERS
We should go . . .
. . . GHOST PEPPER HUNTING!!!
GHOST PEPPER HUNTERS

Chapter 4
Ghost Pepper Hunting

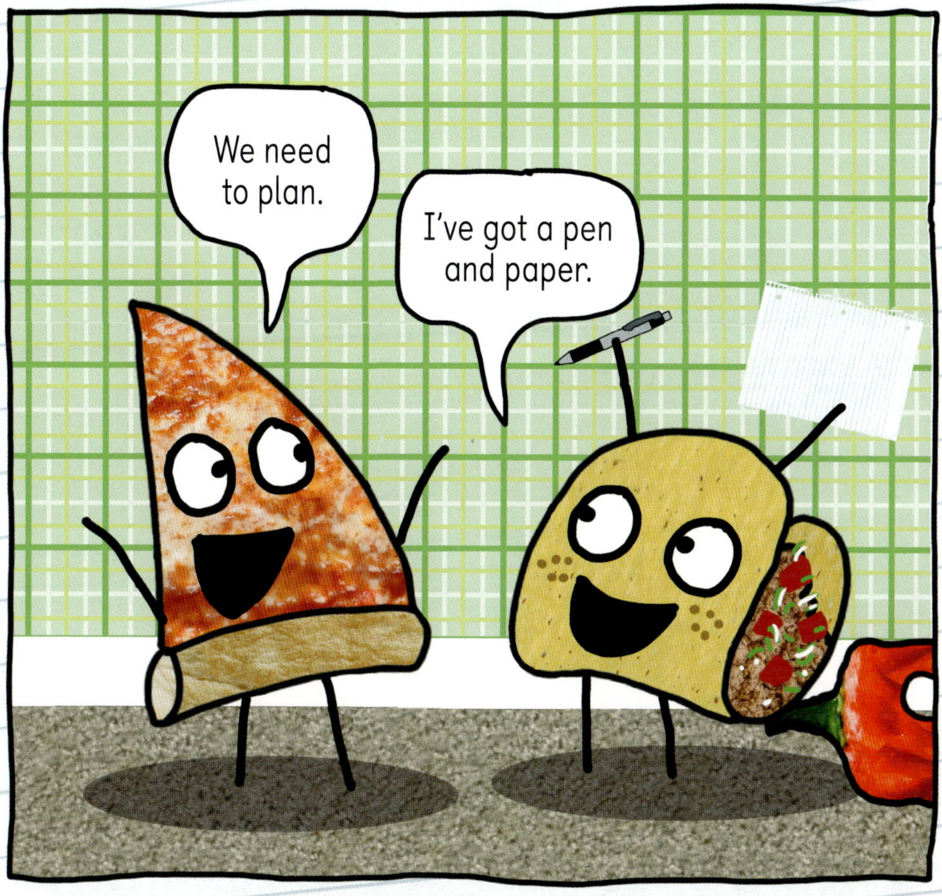
We need to plan.
I've got a pen and paper.

It's got to be dark.
Check!
We need a graveyard.
There's one right by Hot Dog's house.
Check!
What about flashlights?

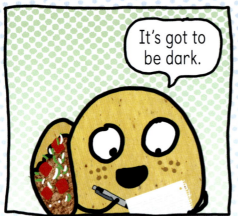

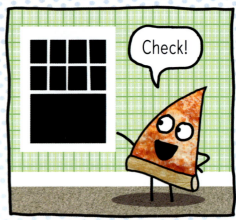

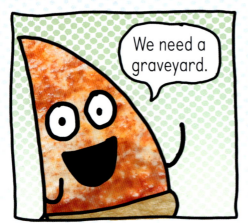

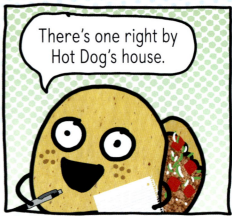

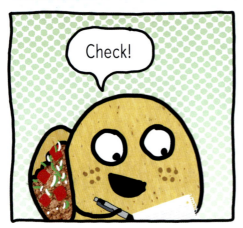

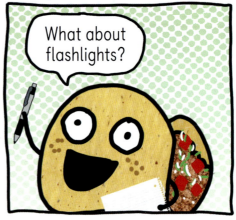

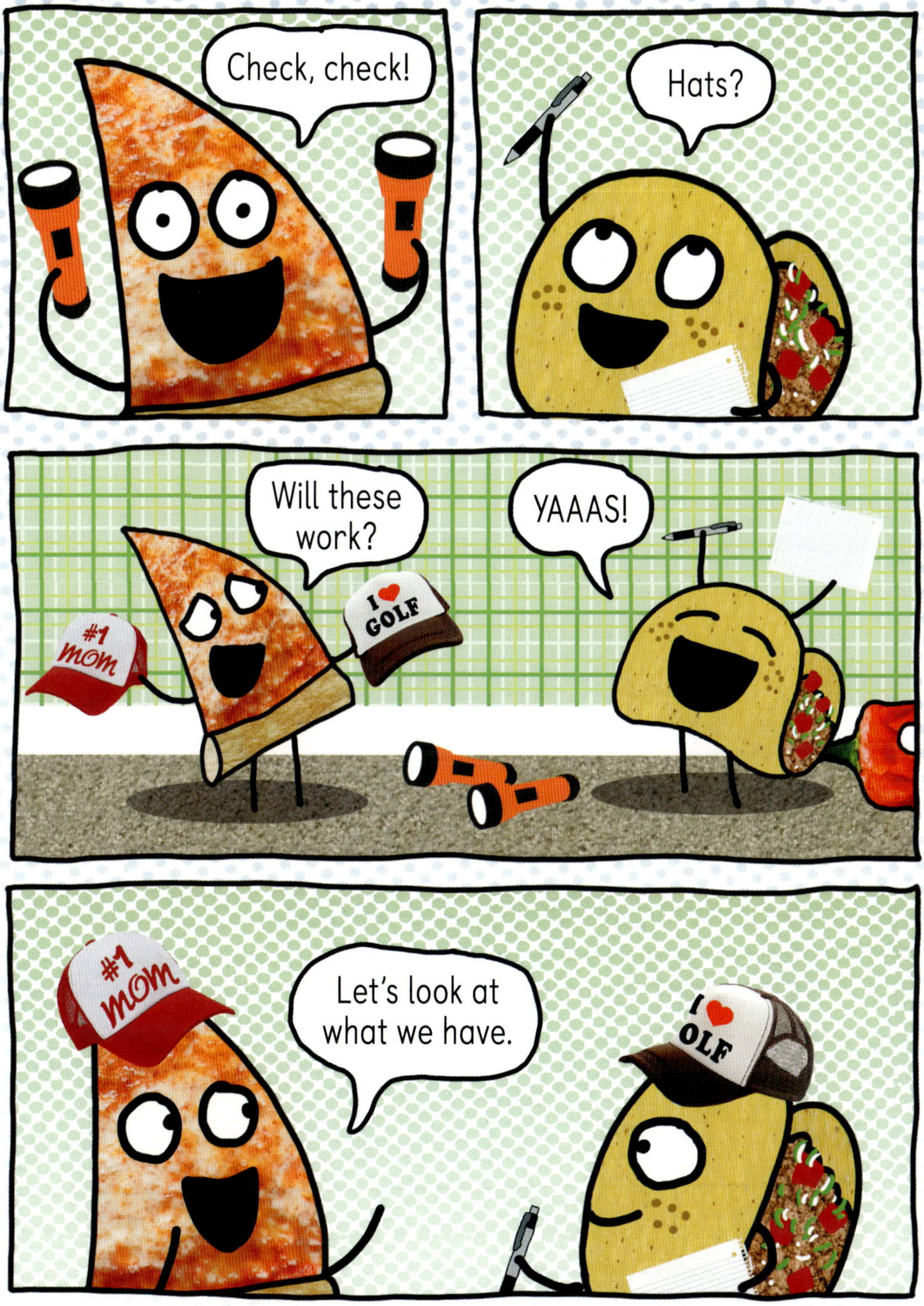
Check, check!
Hats?
Will these work?
#1 MOM
I ♥ GOLF
YAAAS!
Let's look at what we have.
#1 MOM
I ♥ OLF

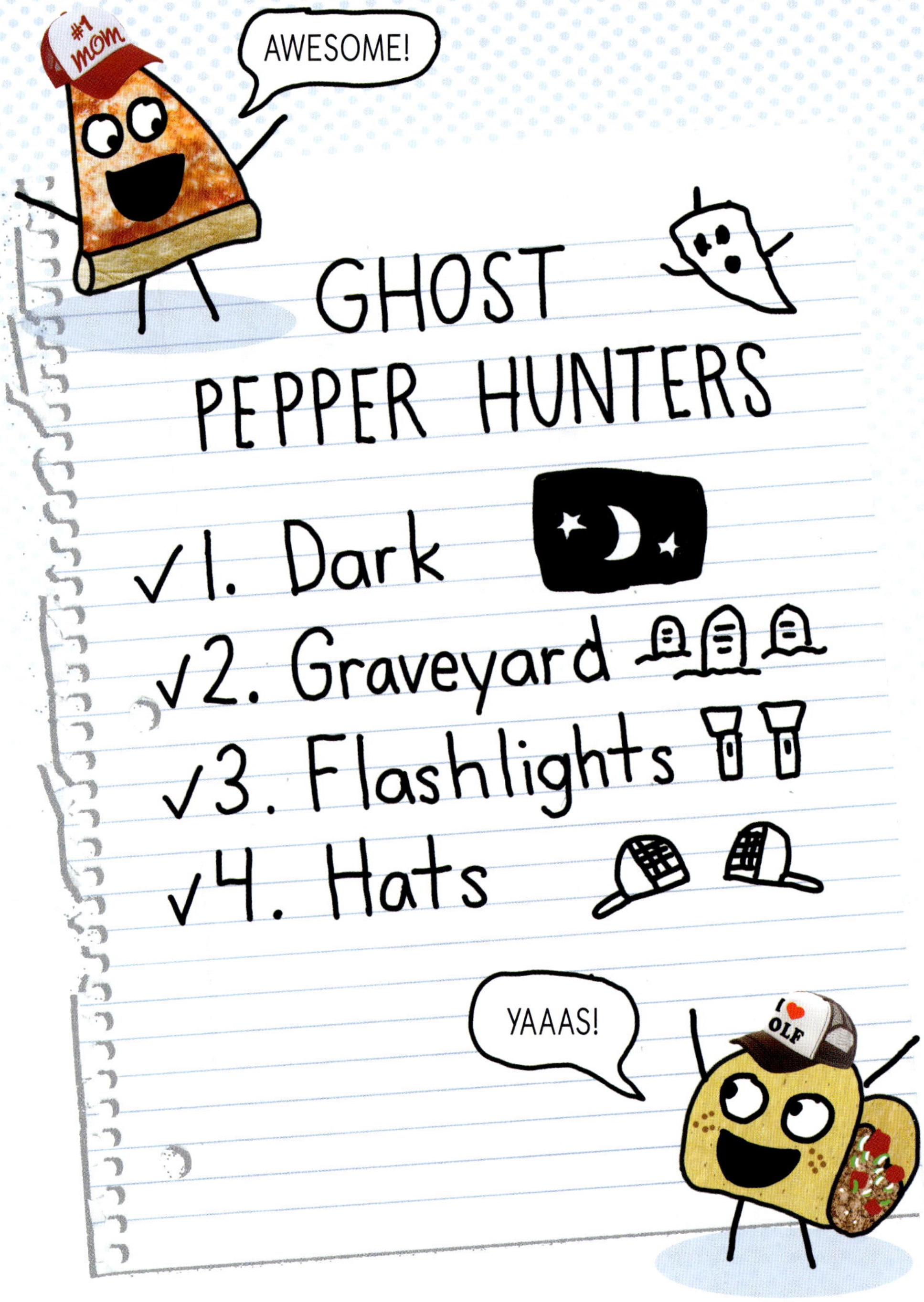

#1 MOM
AWESOME!
GHOST PEPPER HUNTERS
✓1. Dark
✓2. Graveyard
✓3. Flashlights
✓4. Hats
YAAAS!

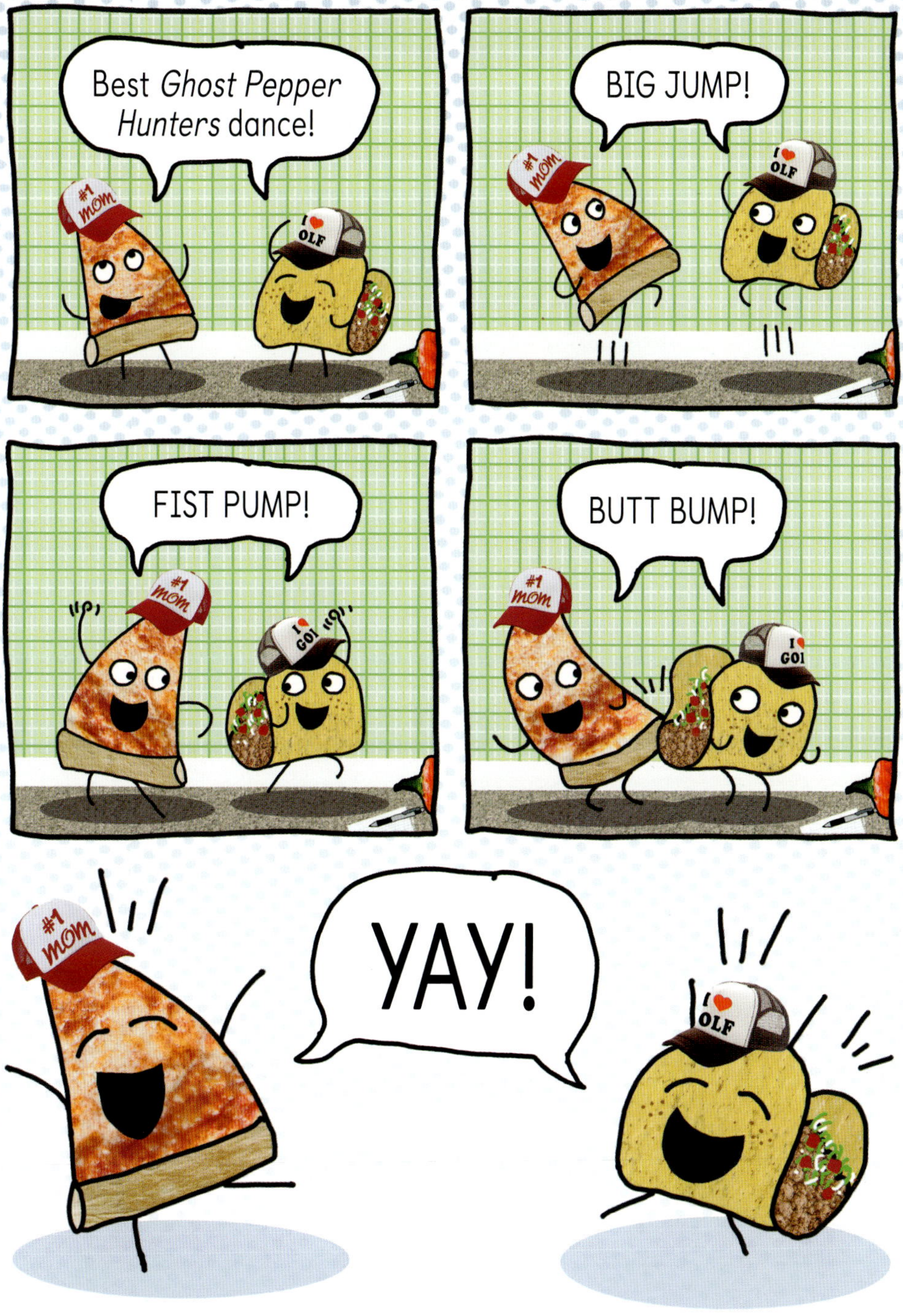
Best *Ghost Pepper Hunters* dance!
#1 MOM
I ♥ OLF
BIG JUMP!
FIST PUMP!
BUTT BUMP!
YAY!

GHOST PEPPERS, BEWARE!
Are you scared?

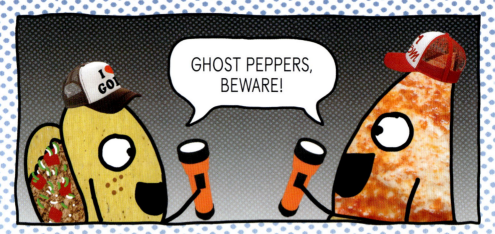

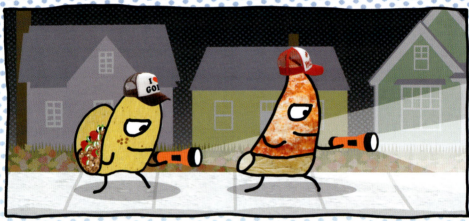

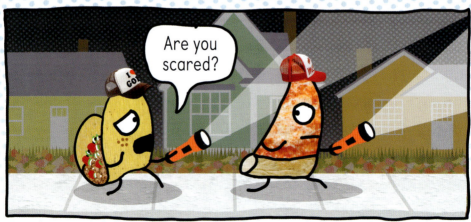

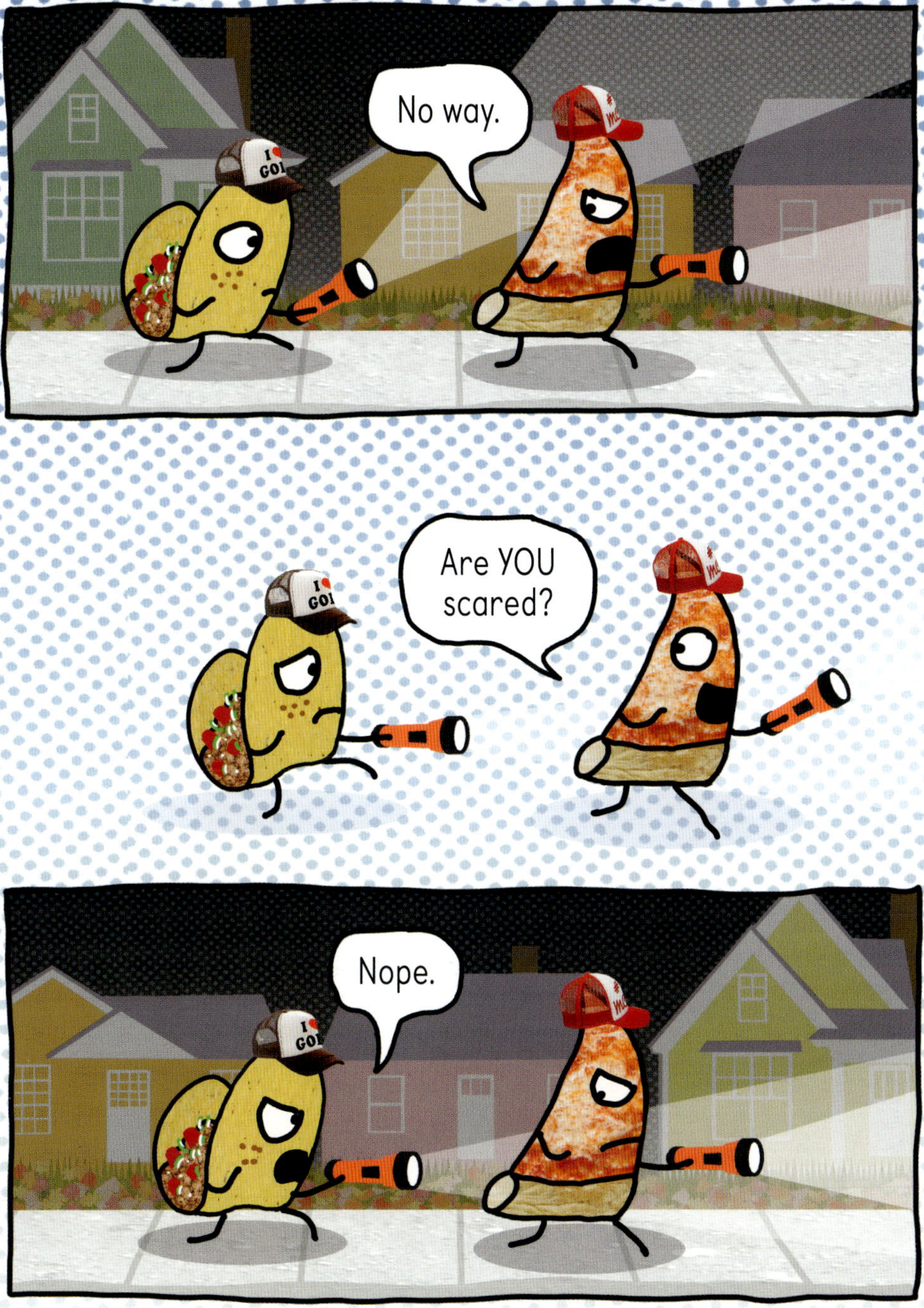
No way.
Are YOU scared?
Nope.

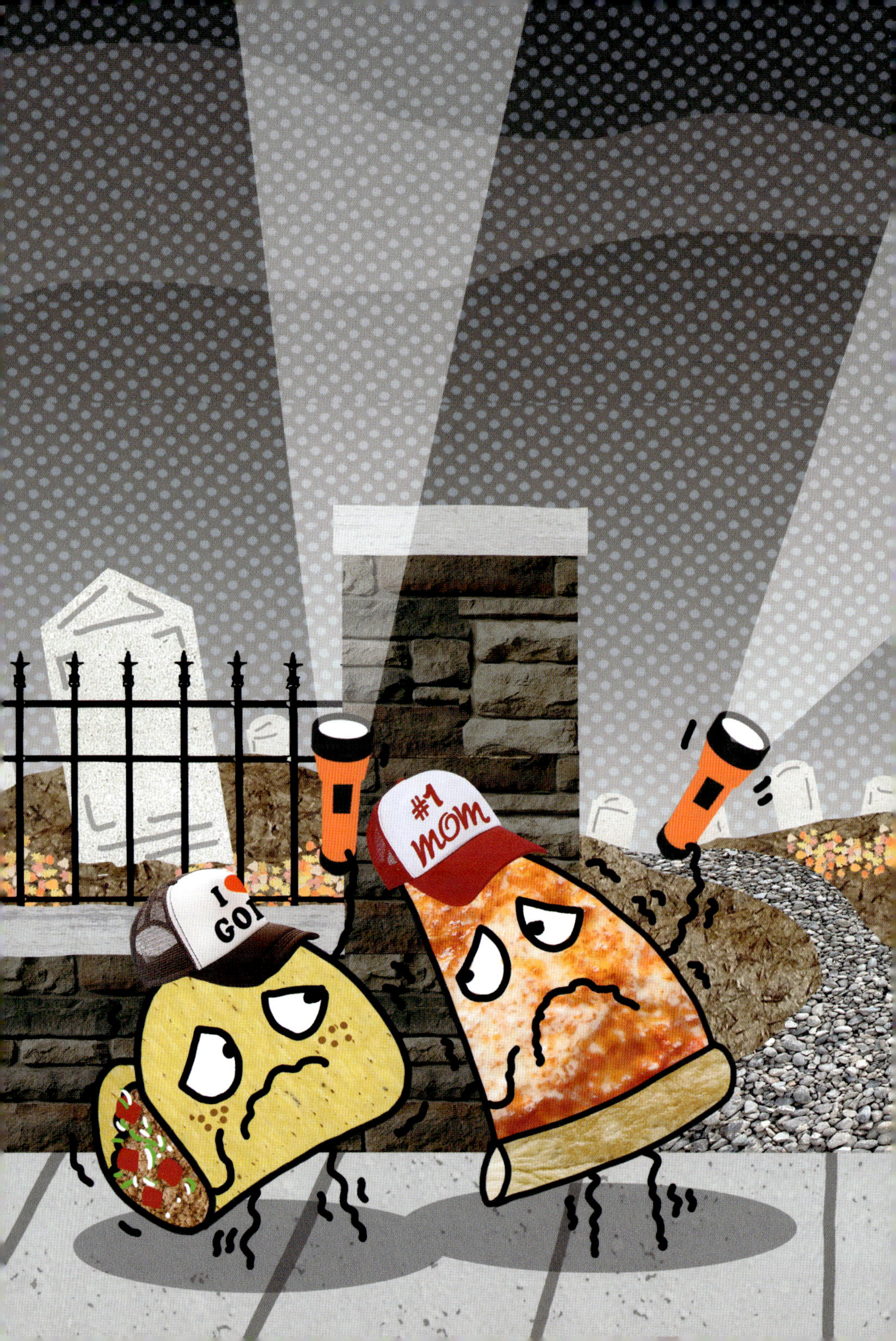
#1
MOM

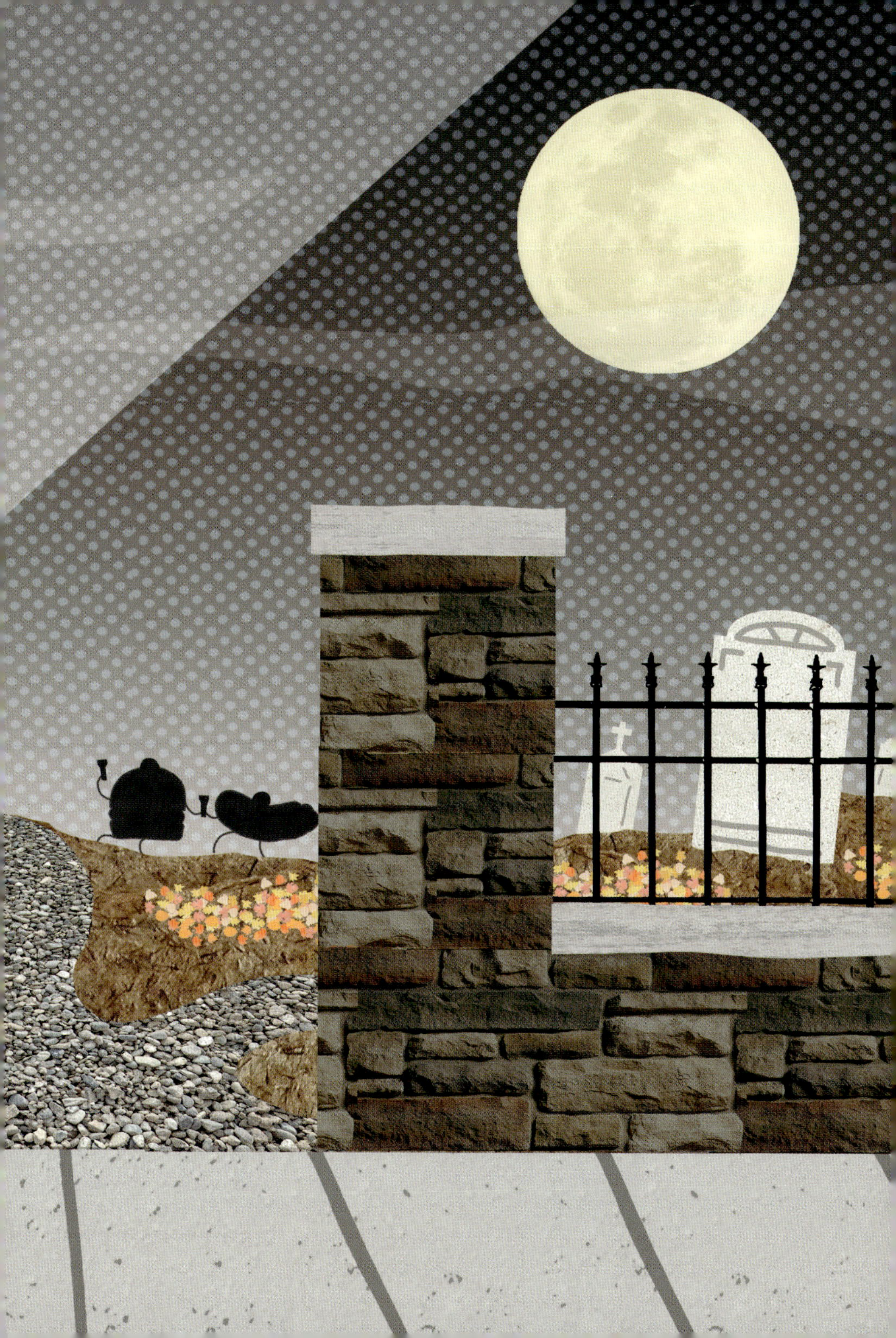

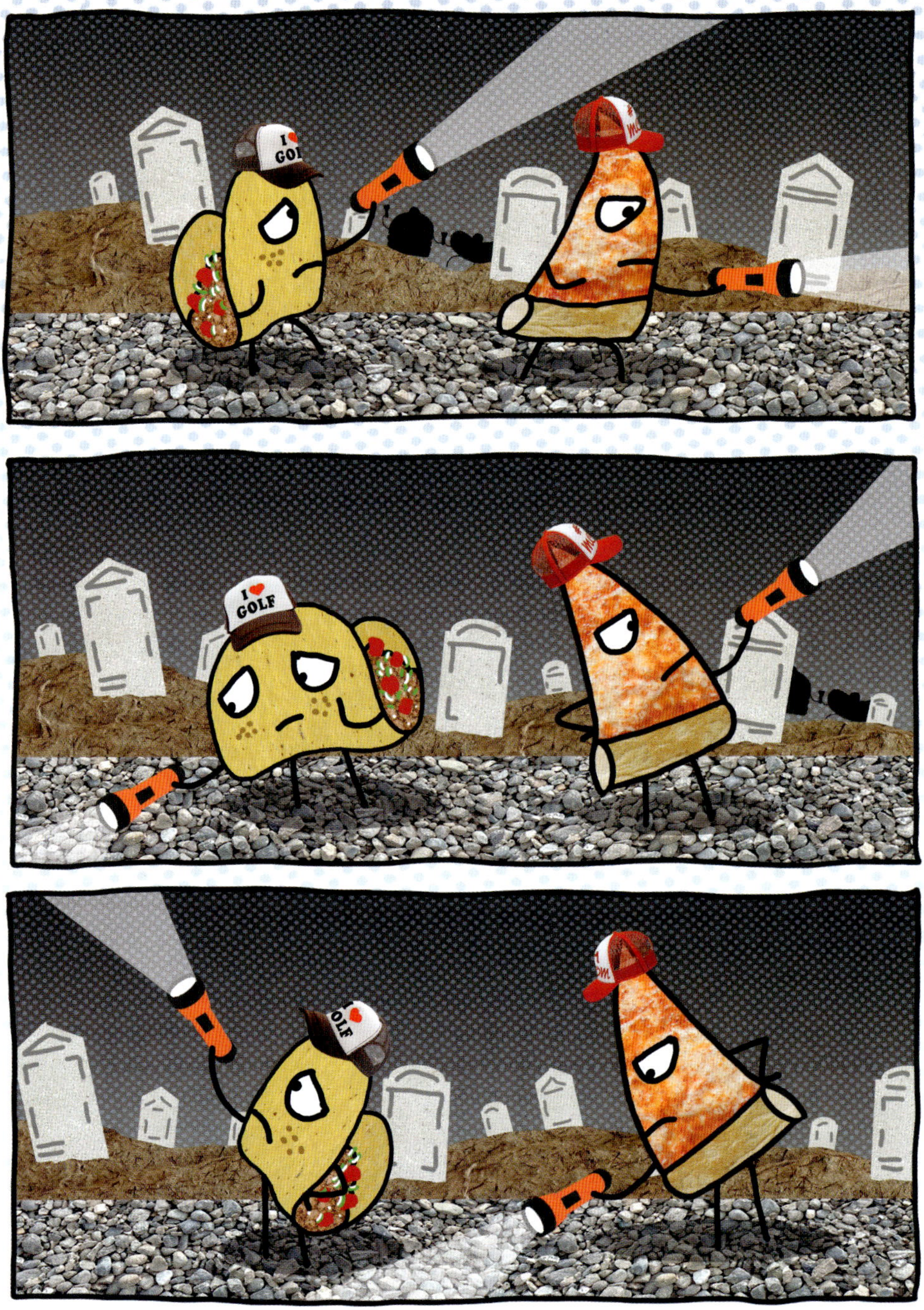
I ♥ GOLF

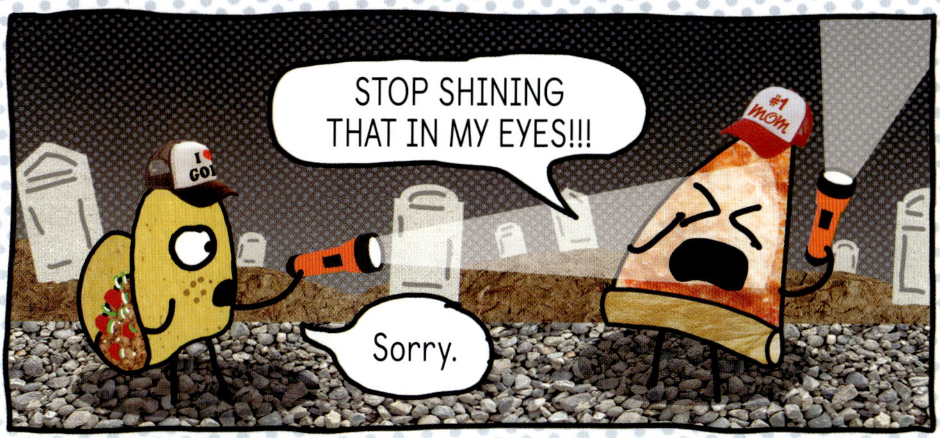
STOP SHINING THAT IN MY EYES!!!
Sorry.

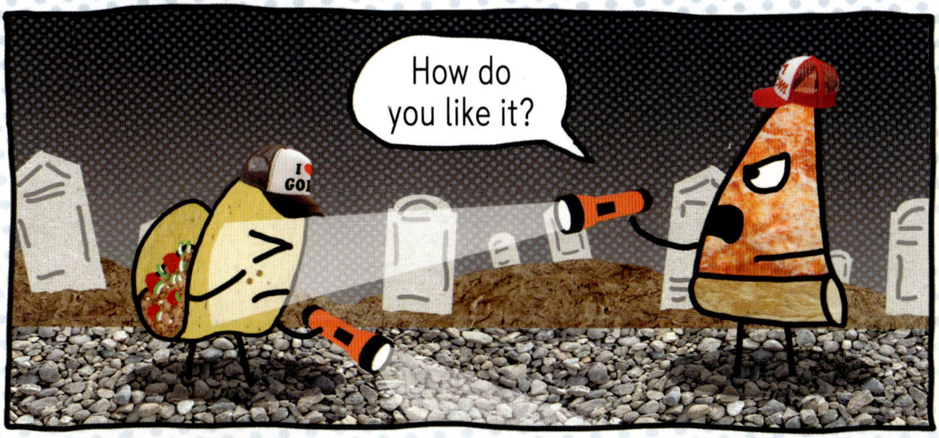
How do you like it?

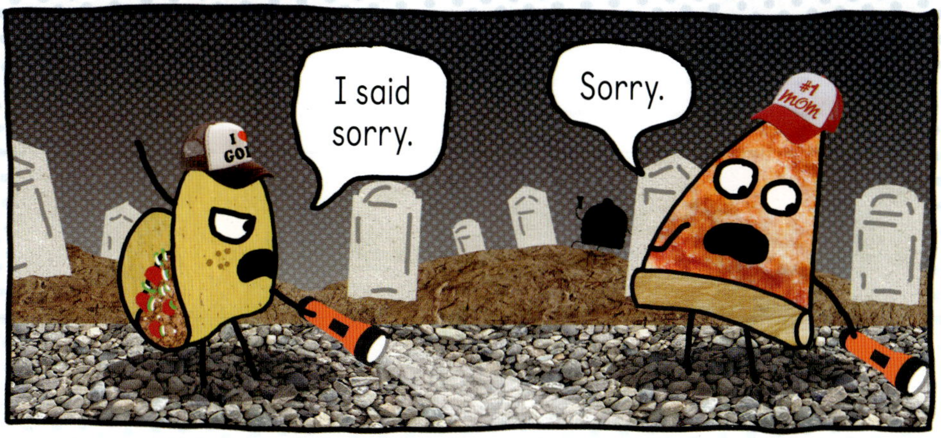
I said sorry.
Sorry.

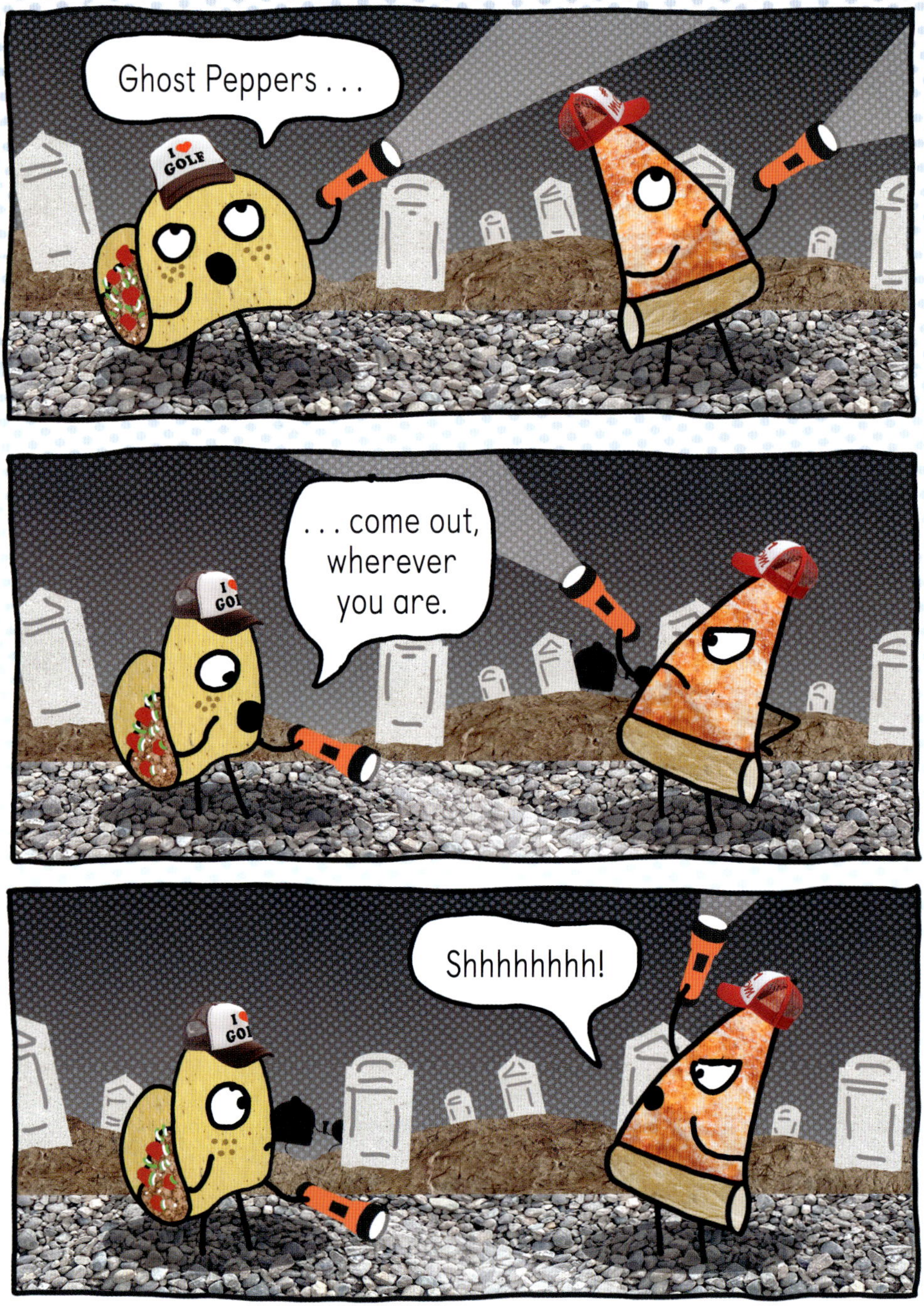
Ghost Peppers . . .
. . . come out, wherever you are.
Shhhhhhhh!

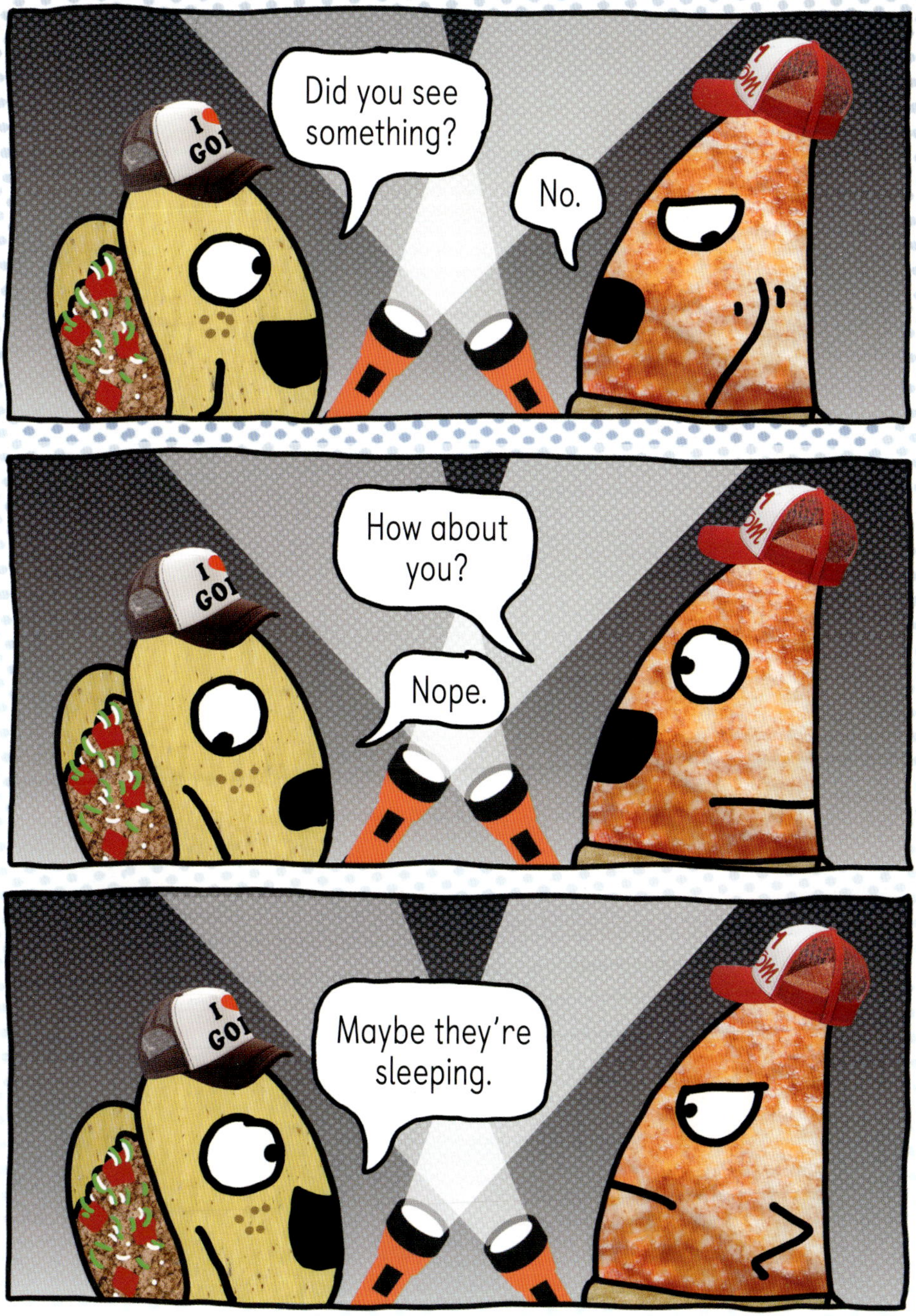
Did you see something?
No.
How about you?
Nope.
Maybe they're sleeping.

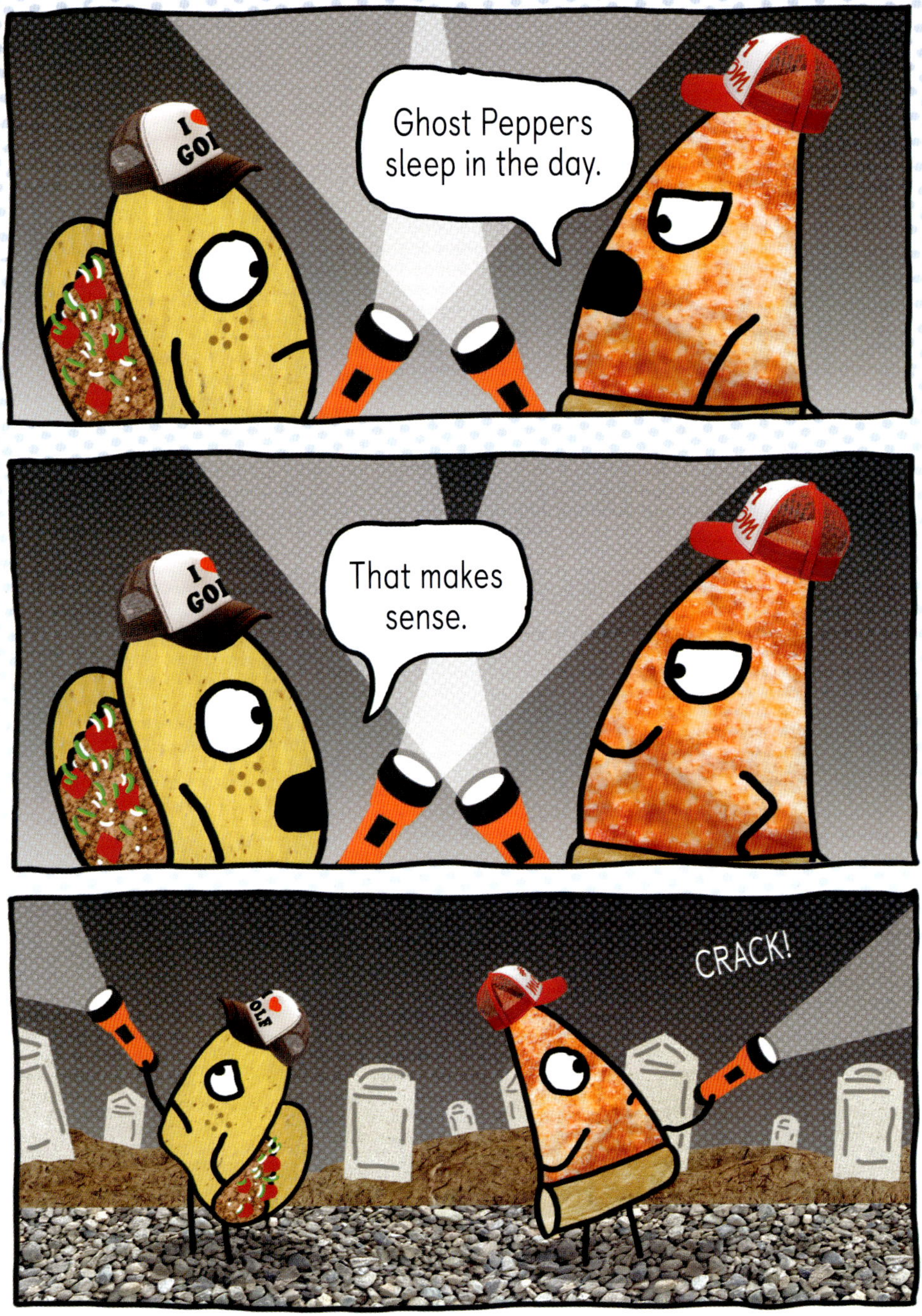
Ghost Peppers sleep in the day.
That makes sense.
CRACK!

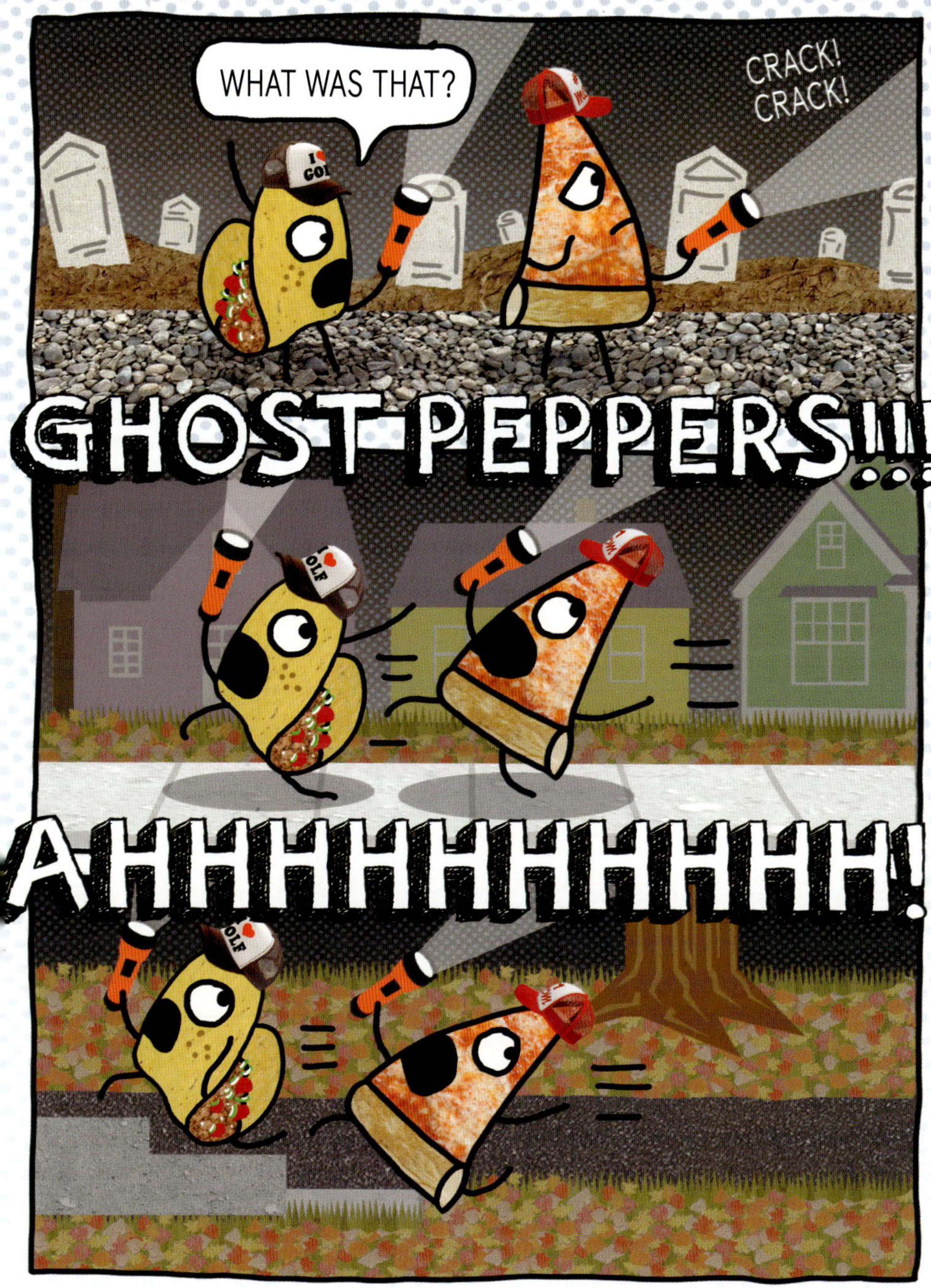
WHAT WAS THAT?
CRACK!
CRACK!
GHOST PEPPERS!!!
AHHHHHHHHHHHH!

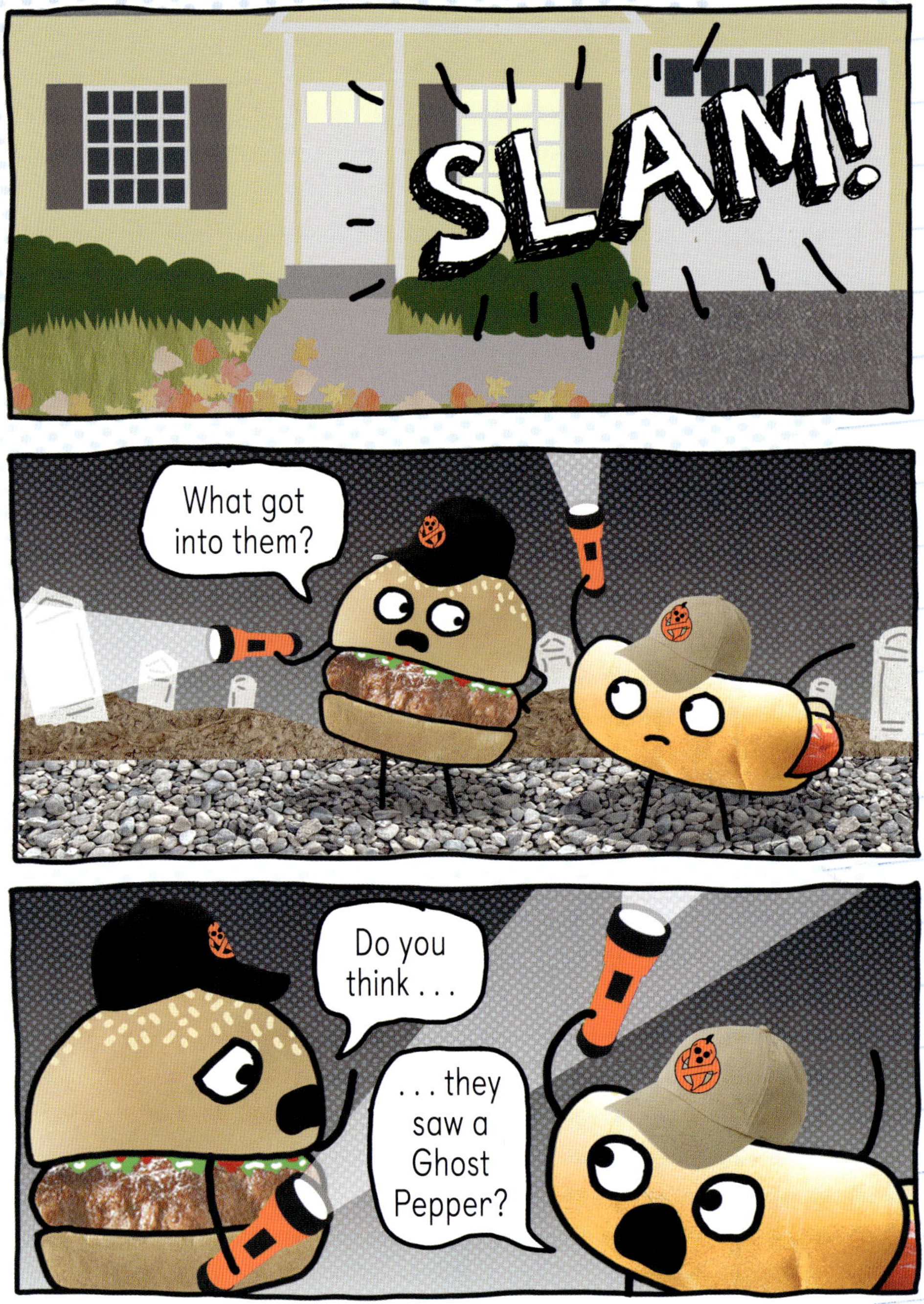
SLAM!
What got into them?
Do you think . . .
. . . they saw a Ghost Pepper?

Chapter 5
We're Not Scared

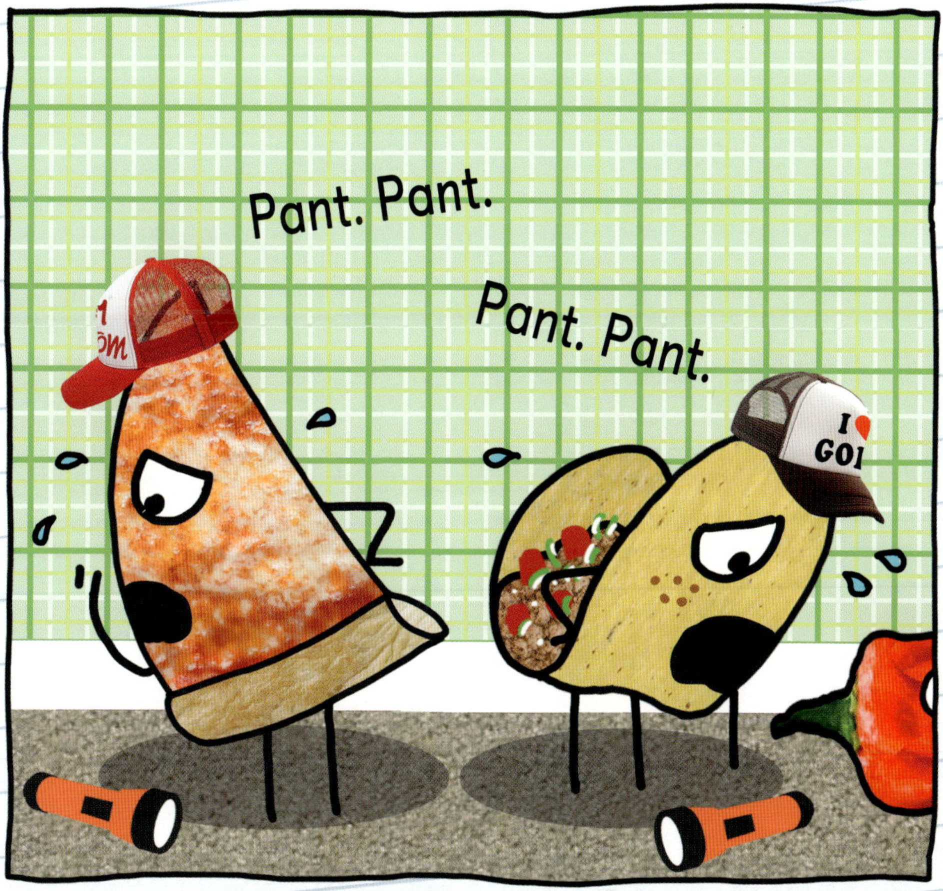

Pant. Pant.
Pant. Pant.

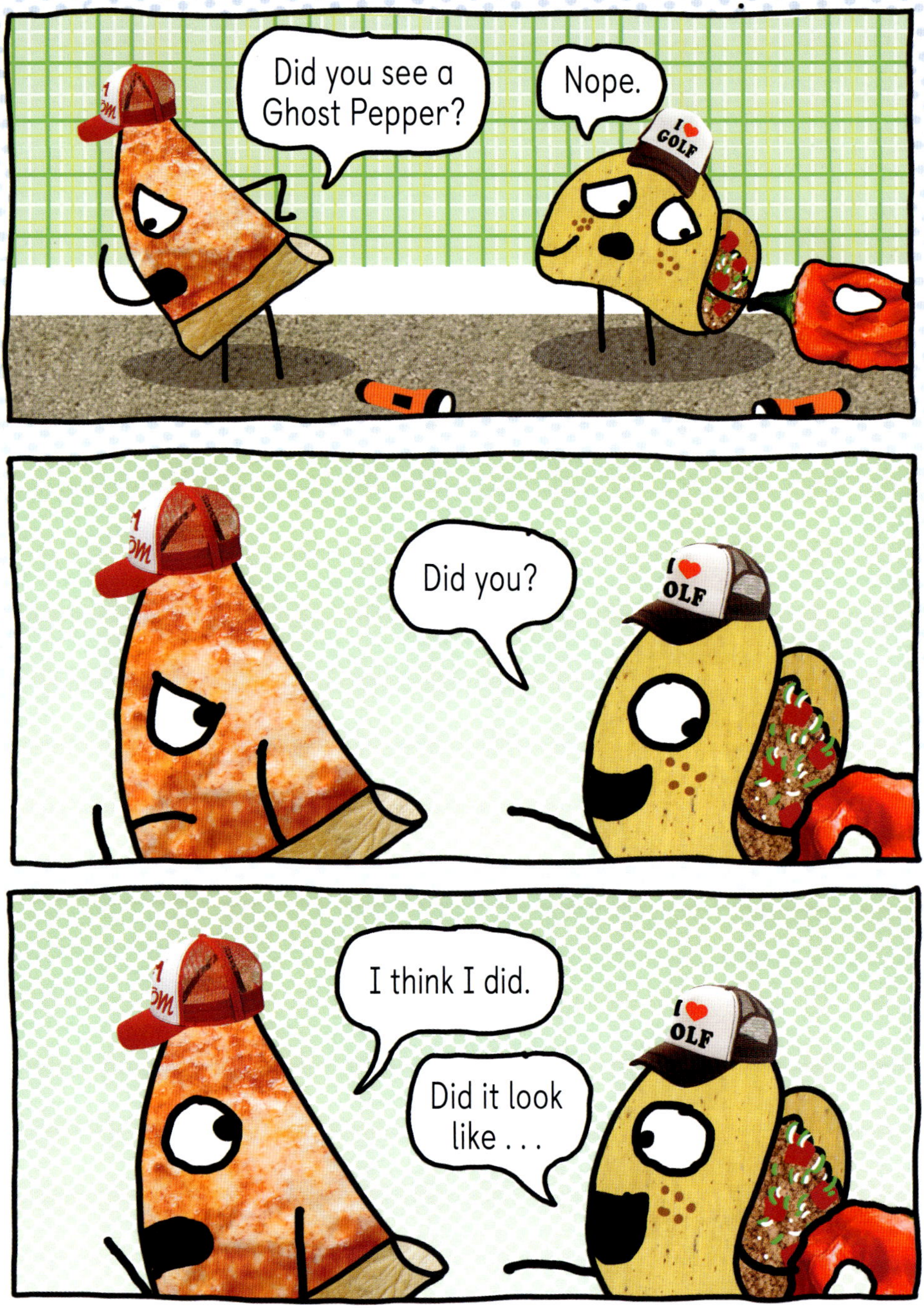
Did you see a Ghost Pepper?
Nope.
I ♥ GOLF
Did you?
I think I did.
Did it look like . . .

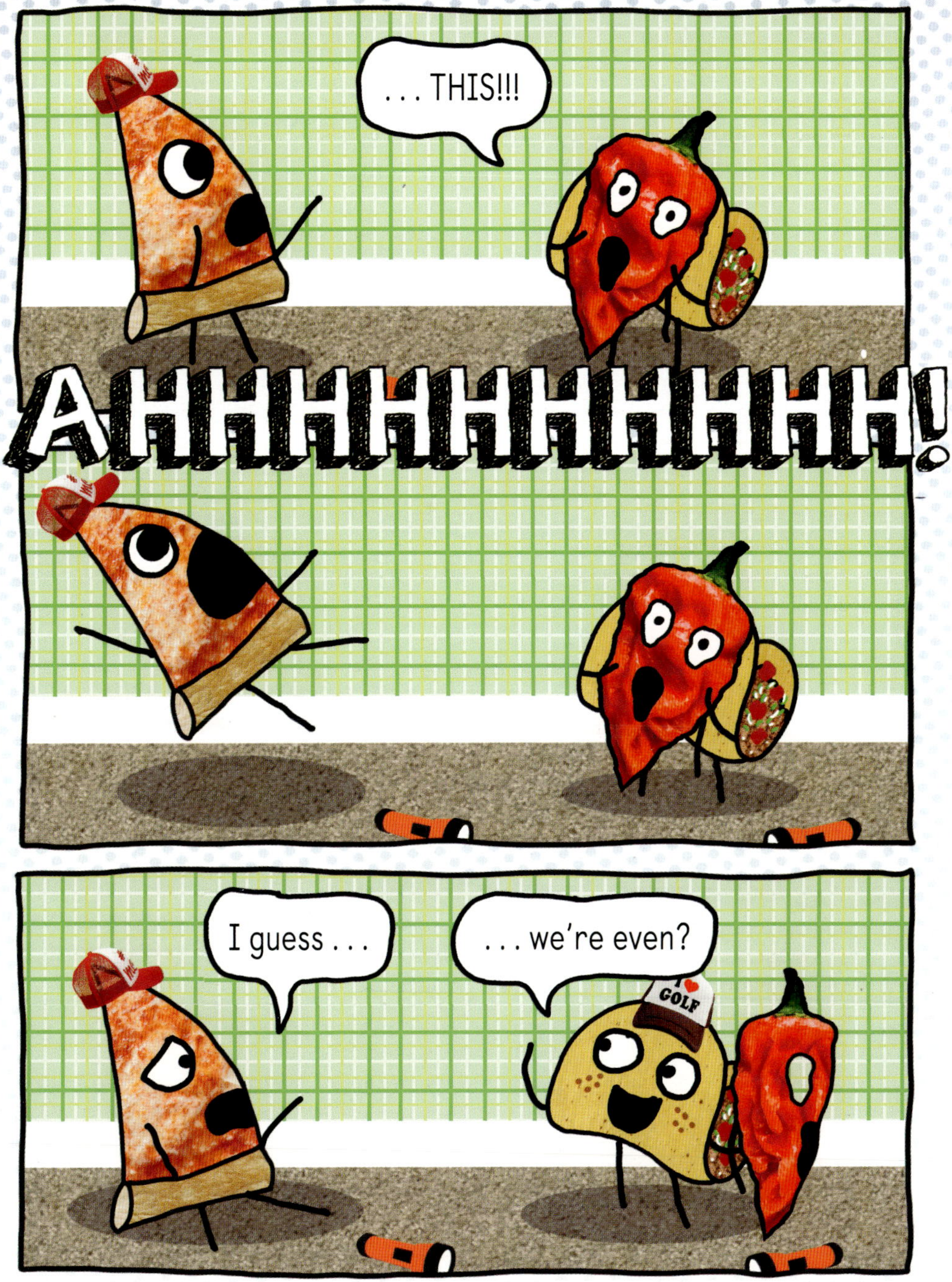
. . . THIS!!!
AHHHHHHHHHHHH!
I guess . . .
. . . we're even?
GOLF

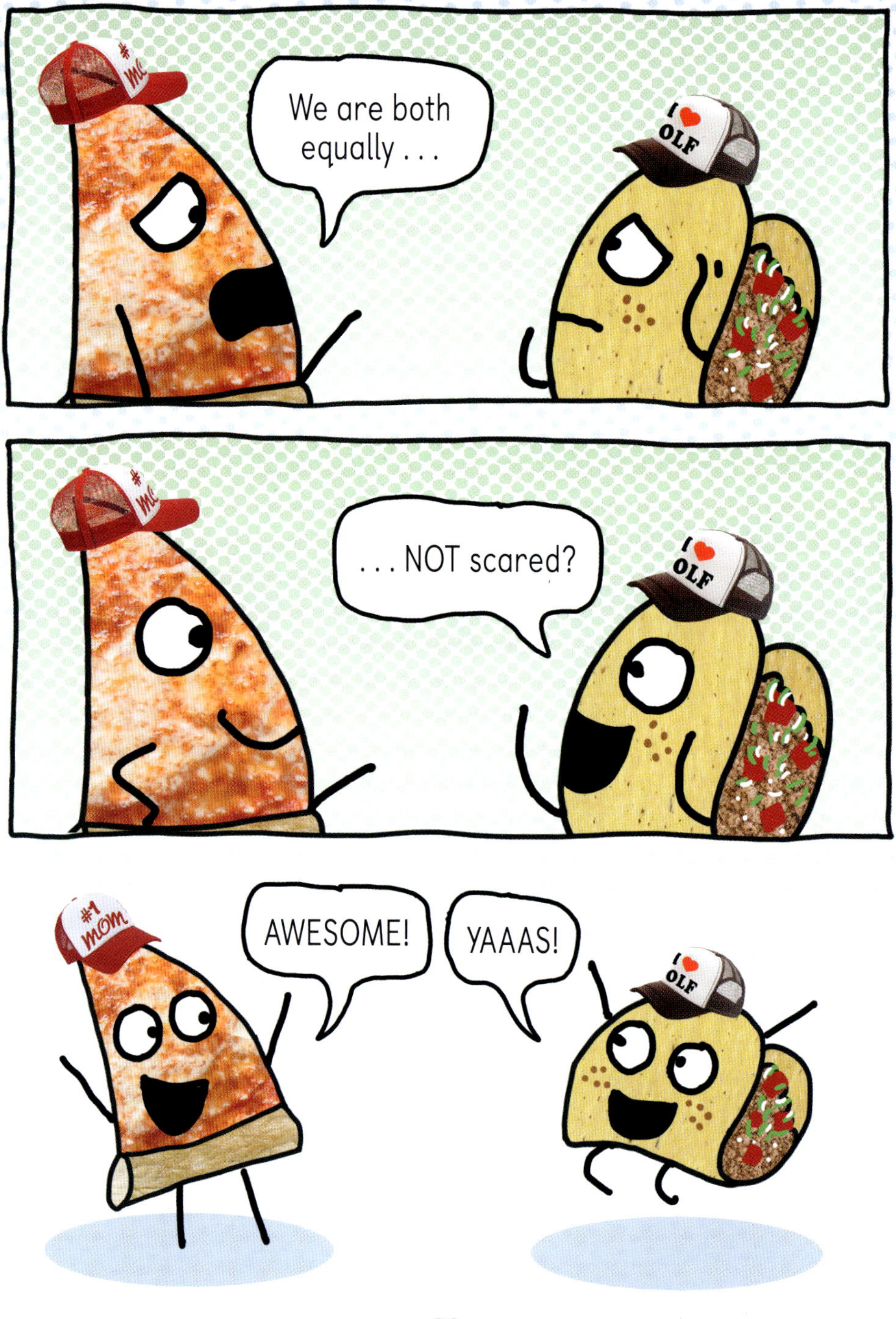
We are both equally . . .
. . . NOT scared?
#1 MOM
AWESOME!
YAAAS!

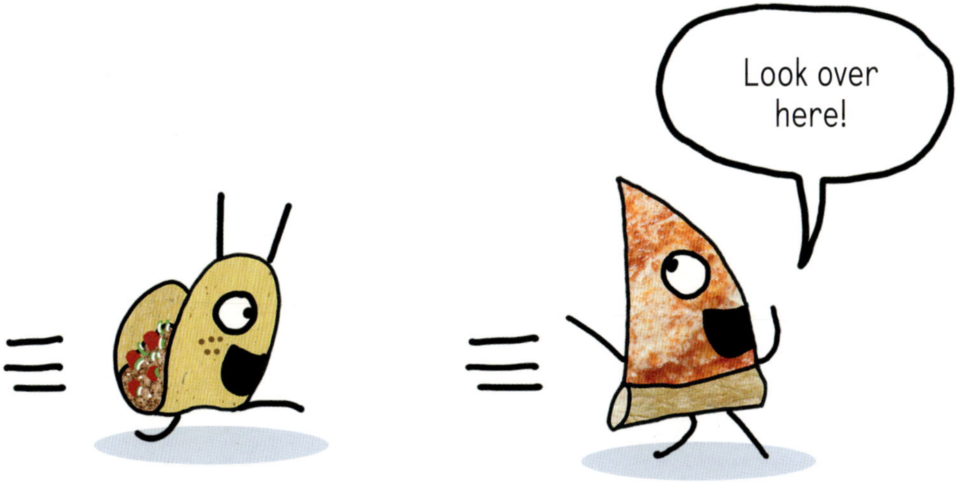
Look over here!

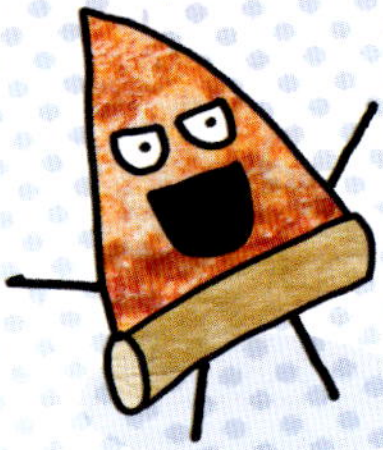

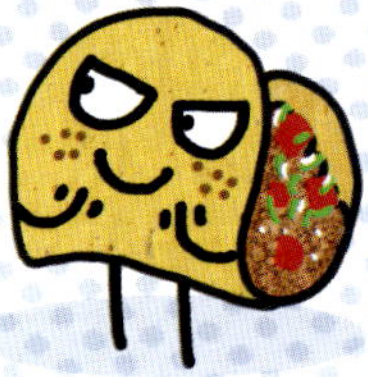

ARE YOU READY TO THROW DOWN WITH PIZZA AND TACO?

PIZZA AND TACO THINK EXERCISE IS OVERRATED.

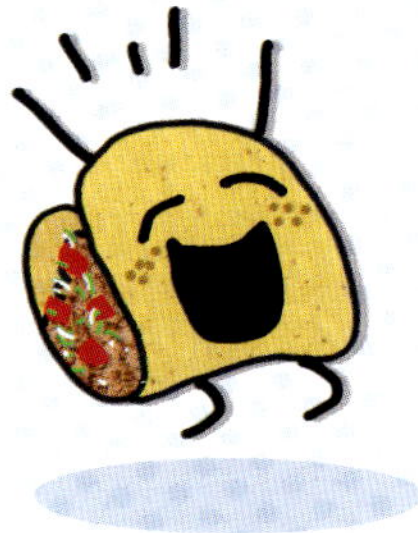

But WRESTLING is going to be COOL!

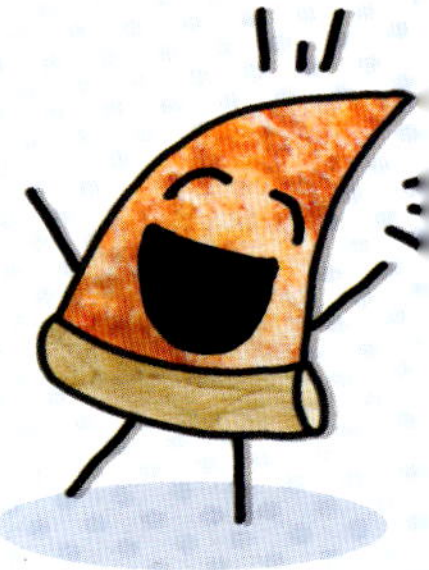

PIZZA AND TACO: WRESTLING MANIA!

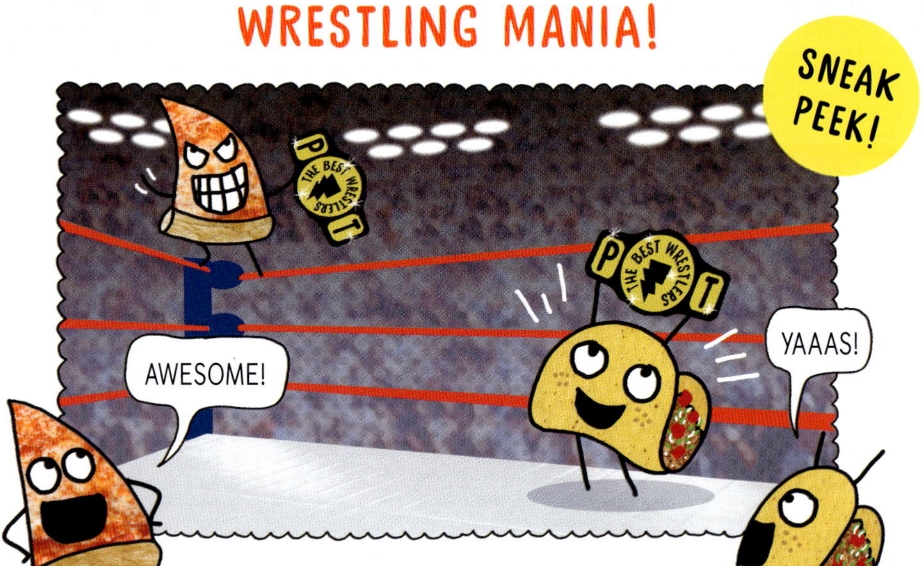

SNEAK PEEK!
THE BEST WRESTLERS
AWESOME!
YAAAS!

Coming in January 2024!

AWESOME COMICS!
AWESOME KIDS!

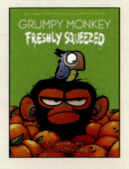

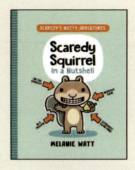

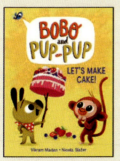

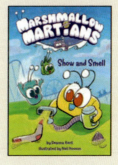

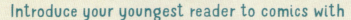

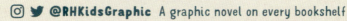

Introduce your youngest reader to comics with

RH GRAPHIC

@RHKidsGraphic A graphic novel on every bookshelf